DRIFTING BETWEEN
EMPTY TRAMLINES

Also by Susan Noble

Before and After the Darkness

Collected Poems

The Dream of Stairs: A Poem Cycle

A Flock of Blackbirds

Inside the Stretch of My Heart

DRIFTING BETWEEN EMPTY TRAMLINES

A Chronicle of Bridchester

Susan Noble

AESOP Modern
Oxford

AESOP Modern
An imprint of AESOP Publications
Martin Noble Editorial / AESOP
28 Abberbury Road, Oxford OX4 4ES, UK
www.aesopbooks.com

Edited from a typescript written in 1972.
First paperback edition published by AESOP Publications
Copyright (c) 2014 The Estate of Susan Noble

ISBN: 978-1-910301-07-4

CONTENTS

CONTENTS

Preface

About the book

Drifting Between Empty Tramlines is a novel about quietly – and not so quietly – desperate women.

Subtitled *A Chronicle of Bridchester*, it is a moral and social satire in the tradition of Jane Austen, focusing on the lives of a group of twenty-something women in the fictional town of Bridchester near Hull in the East Riding of Yorkshire in the 1970s. It was written in 1972 by my sister, Susan Noble, who died in 1974 at the age of 31.

During the late 1960s and early 1970s, Susan worked in London, first at the Royal National Institute for the Blind and later at the National Central Library. Like the Bridchester Records Office in the novel, the NCL – based in Store Street, not far from the British Museum Library – was not open to the public, but was essentially the official clearing house for inter-library lending as part of what was to become, in 1973, the British Library.

The atmosphere of the fictional records office, with its gossip and backbiting, was almost certainly based on that of Susan's daily working life; the office forms the backdrop to the social, cultural, intellectual and emotional concerns of the central characters who grapple with a range of issues from mental illness to marriage and motherhood, their relationships, affairs and break-ups, their preoccupations over work and creativity, conflicts between feminism and traditional family roles, and between academia and 'lived experience'. And above all, throughout the novel, the question of what they should be doing with their lives.

While it is not difficult to see traces of Austen, *Drifting Between Empty Tramlines* also has elements of *Bildungsroman* and novels of ideas. The main protagonists – Anna, Margot, Paula, Alison, Dana and June – embody some of the defining concerns and issues for women during the tumultuous period of transition between the 1950s and 1970s, but in a much more autobiographical sense, each of these characters strikingly reflects different aspects of Susan's own personality. There are also intense moments of the kinds of spiritual perception and longing that may be found in her poems. Ultimately, though, the lives of all the characters are, in different ways, subverted by the same sense of motivational uncertainty as that vividly expressed in the novel's title.

Susan's output of fiction and poetry in the final ten years of her life was prolific and to mark the fortieth anniversary of her death, *Drifting Between Empty Tramlines* is being published in hardback, paperback and ebook for the first time, along with four companion volumes of her poetry, *The Dream of Stairs: A Poem Cycle; Inside the Stretch of My Heart; Before and After the Darkness*; and *Collected Poems*, as well as a selection of her short stories and novellas, *A Flock of Blackbirds*.

Profits from the sales of all six volumes are being donated to three charities: Mind, the Samaritans and Sane. For more details, see page xi. Facsimiles of the original typescripts and manuscripts are available online at:

www.aesopbooks.com/susannoble

Martin Noble
Oxford, 2014

About the author

Brought up in South London, my sister, Susan Noble, was the second of three children. Her childhood was enriched by being part of our large and closely-knit Jewish family. Unfortunately stricken by polio (then known as infantile paralysis) in her early years, Susan went through life with a degree of physical handicap which she was to overcome with courage and determination.

Educated at Croydon High School, Susan studied English at Somerville College, Oxford. After graduating, Susan worked in London, first at the Royal National Institute for the Blind, dictating books for transcription into Braille, and later at the National Central Library in London, where she qualified as a Chartered Librarian.

Susan's exceptional sensitivity was reflected not only in the intense outpouring of poems to be found in *The Dream of Stairs, Inside the Stretch of My Heart*, and *Before and After the Darkness*, but also in the novel *Drifting Between Empty Tramlines* and the short story collection *A Flock of Blackbirds*. In both her poetry and her fiction, she chronicles her personal response to the world around her, while vividly portraying the inner landscape of her own mental and emotional struggle.

Judith Frankel
Netanya, 2014

Susan Noble

One's first impression of Susan was of fragility. She was an acutely sensitive person, but her physical and emotional fragility really masked a very great spiritual strength.

Her sensitivity indeed was not directed only towards herself, but towards others. She was sensitive to the needs of others, and her strength and also perhaps some of her inner conflicts came from a deep desire for goodness which could not be matched in reality by the world as she found it.

Susan passionately wished to be independent; she struggled for it from the time she went to university, and throughout her work as a librarian, and she was able to maintain it to the very end.

There was an intellectual and emotional intensity which burned within her and which predominantly found outward expression in her writing and when she expressed herself thus she did so with great imaginative power and also with an uncompromising honesty and integrity.

The late Rabbi Dr David Goldstein
South London, July 1974

Publisher's note

All profits from the sale of this volume are being donated to the following charities:

The National Association for Mental Health
www.mind.org.uk

www.samaritans.org

www.sane.org.uk

Words pour out. They flutter round me like an army of birds, friendly and stimulating. I am no longer alone, drifting between empty tramlines, frightened of an oncoming train of intellect that will run me over and crush me into blood and pieces of torn flesh. The ideas caress my hair and flutter up and down my arms, each word singing and resounding.

Susan Noble, 'A Break in Time', *A Flock of Blackbirds*

The sun shines down clearly onto the bibliography she is checking. As so often, the lower portion of the page has crumbled away. She gazes at the soft edges where the corner has disappeared. How odd it seems that this edge is not clean-cut but a gradual paring away of the paper. She is suddenly confounded by her consciousness of the minuteness of things. It seems curious that each piece of paper comprises so many tiny particles, that her body is a vast conglomeration of molecules and that the dust, shimmering on the table, is made up of a mixture of minute substances.

It seems that there in no limit to each individual object or person, for if dust can merge, so can fragments and objects and human beings. Why then does she have this wish to be self-sufficient? Is it possible – or even desirable? Just as there is something to be gained from sharing experience and communication, is there also something to be gained from remaining silent and pondering within oneself? After a moment's reflection it occurs to her that the latter state is at most a mere substitute for the former; something to be endured rather than to be sought after. Yet perhaps it is her fate to endure it.

Susan Noble, *Drifting Between Empty Tramlines*

Who's Who in Bridchester

Aileen – Australian, secretary at Bridchester Records Office

Alison Gregory – part-time history student at Hull; secretary to Paula (Assistant Archivist) at Bridchester Records Office; married to Steve

Andrew – student on Alison's part-time history course

Angela Withers-Browne – friend of Margaret Bushnell

Anna Crawley – patient at Bridchester Mental Hospital

Arnold – party guest, friend of Pete's (William's former tutor)

Bert Goodrich – caretaker at Bridchester Records Office

Charles – lover of Deirdre

Colin Phillips – patient at Bridchester Mental Hospital

Cynthia – junior at Bridchester Records Office

Dana Newsom – part-time artist, researcher on biography of the Duke of Bridchester and daughter of Professor Newsom

Deirdre – Paula's flatmate

Douglas Gifford – chartered accountant, Paula's boyfriend

Dr Mueller – consultant at Bridchester Hospital

Father John – priest at St Michael's Catholic Church, Bridchester

Father Peter – blind priest at St Michael's Catholic Church, Bridchester

Fiona – Alison's aunt

George – Alison's uncle

Hilary Harrison – four-and-a-half-year-old daughter of Margot and Tony

Hugh Thomas – student who sharpened a pencil in the Records Office reading room.

Jan Kaminsky – Polish writer; member of writers' circle

Jean – student on Alison's part-time history course

Jenny Ellis – third-year maths student at Hull University, friend of Anna's

John Brent – Jenny's fiancé

Josie – Australian, secretary at Bridchester Records Office

June Brentwood – primary school teacher, later temporary clerk at Bridchester Records Office, married to Tom

Madeleine Mitchell – hostess of writers club meeting

Margaret Bushnell (aka Miss Bushnell, aka Maggie) – Head Archivist at Bridchester Records Office

Margot Harrison – American, secretary in Bridchester, married to Tony

Mike Brennan – journalist on *Bridchester Gazette*, partner of Dana

Molly Enright – Roger's wife

Mrs Anderson – Paula's landlady

Professor Humphrey Newsom – historian at Hull University

Paula Richards – Assistant Archivist at Bridchester Records Office; Douglas's girlfriend

Pete Matthews – William's former sociology tutor at Hull University

Roger Enright – theology lecturer who gives a talk to the local history society

Sally – five-year-old friend of Hilary

Sandra Wilcox – receptionist at Bridchester Records Office

Steve Gregory – insurance broker, married to Alison

Tom Brentwood – historian, lecturer at Hull University, married to June

Tony Harrison – postgraduate student at Hull, revising his thesis, married to Margot

William Pearce – dropout sociology student, temporary clerk at Bridchester Records Office

Prologue

HE GREEN and blue chips of stone lie in a scattered heap on the table in front of Anna Crawley as she swivels the vase around between her hands. She has already covered the lower portion with the chips and the top part looks strangely naked without the uneven bulk of the chips. She dips a long, blue slither into the glue and sticks it onto the top area of the vase with gentle care. It stands out incongruously among the large expanse of brown china.

Anna gazes at it and wonders what adjectives could best describe it. She considers the words 'solitary', 'aloof' and 'absurd'. Then it occurs to her that all three adjectives could equally apply to herself in her present predicament.

Today is one of her better days and in the calm silence of the morning, she feels more able to organise her thoughts than usual. And the tranquillisers she has been given at breakfast have chased away the whispering voices that often disturb her thoughts and make it difficult for her to form logical sequences of reasoning.

Dr Gordon has told her that the voices she hears are due to a disassociation of consciousness, but when she looked this phrase up in a dictionary and quoted her opinions on it to him, he looked displeased, and she felt a barrier arise between them, as though a veil had fallen between their lines of communication. Since then she has been feeling more isolated and uneasy.

Even so, despite the fact that she is now labelled as mentally ill and her freedom is restricted, she is much happier than she was last year, when she was still struggling in the world outside. At that time she was in her second year at Hull University and her essay-writing had become more and more difficult. Her visits to the theatre, coffee meetings, dinner parties, and other social gatherings were clouded by a morass of violent but confused emotions, which destroyed both her enjoyment and understanding of what was going on around her.

Finally, she had informed her tutor that she did not feel like studying any more. She is now able to recognise that her consciousness of external reality was – and still is – fractured and distorted. Now everything is so much clearer and more straightforward. She no longer has to pretend to be like everyone else, but can sit back and relax, drifting between the empty tramlines of her non-life.

When her voices come, they seem to bring with them the reward of an extra amount of sympathy and affection, for when she describes in detail her mental and emotional experiences to the doctors and nurses and after listening patiently for half an hour, nodding their heads in understanding, they show their empathy at the conclusion of the weekly meetings by stepping up her medication doses accordingly.

The only thing that frightens her is that her occasional sallies into the outside world are becoming less and less frequent and more and more difficult. No-one except herself understands this predicament and although she continually nags at the doctors for permission to be allowed out for the occasional lecture or visit to church, they do not realise that she does this as an act of duty to herself. She needs to reassure herself that she can still master her will-power and has not become weakened by what she terms to herself the pampering of the hospital, and what everybody else terms the necessary treatment.

It is in this conflict of wanting to remain protected, yet forcing herself to be independent, that Anna feels so isolated and because of her inability to communicate these thoughts to anyone, she feels alone and aloof from the rest of the world.

She looks again at the single piece of green stone. Not only is she isolated and aloof, but she is absurd. She does not know why, but she is. There is no denying it, and as this thought strikes her, she laughs very loudly, so that everyone else in the occupational therapy hut ceases their work and looks up in surprise.

A nurse walks over to her. 'Are you all right, Anna? Are you feeling all right in yourself today?'

Anna continues to laugh, trying to modify the noise but unable to, so that it doubles in volume.

'Yes,' she says, 'it's just so funny.'

The nurse smiles. 'I'm glad you're feeling happy today, dear. What a pretty vase. And what lovely colours. Did you do it all by yourself?'

'Yes,' Anna gasps, wiping a tear out of her eyes that has welled up as usual during one of her laughing fits.

'Well, that's very pretty. We'll have to put it in our display next month, won't we?'

1

Searchroom and Enquiries

THE LIGHT is fading as Tom walks through the side streets of Bridchester in search of the Records Office. Eventually he finds it, a large, shabby block of offices, decorated like a cheap wedding cake with fussy crenellations, which on closer inspection turn out to be rows of tiny window boxes.

It is seven o'clock: he only has half an hour in which to see round the place. He enters; walks through a long corridor, lined with notices, rules and regulations; turns up a narrow flight of stairs and finds himself in front of a dull green painted door. The paint is flaking and stuck in the middle on a faded manila sheet of paper is written in an exaggerated attempt at artistry:

Bridchester Local Records Office
Searchroom and Enquiries

He knocks tentatively and entered. A tall brunette in black maxi-skirt and white blouse is standing by a desk in the corner, flicking over the pages of a folder with a bored expression on her face. She looks up in annoyance.

'Yes?'

'I just thought I'd like to have a look round the search-room,' he says politely.

'Well, we haven't got anyone here officially to show you round now. You should have rung earlier and made an appointment.'

'I did ring today, and I was told you were open to the public until 7.30 on Thursdays.'

'Well, we are, but it's just that we don't have anyone here at the moment to take you round.'

'Oh, I see. Well, that doesn't matter. I only wanted to have a quick glance round... out of interest.'

'Oh, all right. Would you like to see the visitors' book?'

She hands him a large book in which he writes '*Thomas Brentwood*', and under 'Occupation', '*Lecturer in History at Hull University*'.

Seeing this, she relents a little. 'Oh, my name's Sandra – Sandra Wilcox. I'm taking a part-time degree in history.'

'Are you? It must be quite hard work doing it part-time.'

'Well, it takes a lot of organising,' she replies. 'Have you been here before?'

'No, I regret to say I haven't. I suddenly realised last week that I ought to become better acquainted with this place in case I need to consult it for my researches.'

'Well, here's an introductory leaflet,' she says, 'and here's a guide to the records we hold. It's quite well arranged, actually. Anyway, do look around and get to know our index and reference books.'

'Thanks very much.'

It occurs to Tom that her attitude towards him has quickly changed from sullen indifference to friendly interest. She reminds him of June, with her quick temper and sudden, warm reconciliations. Tom likes to think that he regards most of the human race with good-natured, placid equanimity, even if June sometimes makes this difficult for him.

He wanders slowly around the bookshelves, most of them filled with large tomes bound in red or black leather, and some of the latter tooled in gold. He picks up a catalogue of the archives held in the collection, his eyes idly picking on such titles as 'Pauper Removal Orders', 'Sessions of the Peace Registers' and 'Turnpike Trust Accounts and Deeds'.

He looks at his watch: only another few minutes before they close. These archives have been here for centuries and will still be there next time he comes, but his dinner won't wait, and he has no idea what kind of mood June will be in.

For Tom, history and historical artefacts are so much easier to understand than people in general, and June in particular. But at least, he thinks, she will have his dinner ready for him.

2

Margot in the Morning

MARGOT Harrison wipes the kitchen worktop with a cloth, wrings it out and looks in the mirror, which is fixed askew between the continental teacloth and an animal calendar presented to them last year by an aunt of Tony's, who spends much of her spare time doing voluntary work for the RSPCA.

As she inspects herself, she automatically winces and immediately adjusts her features. It is odd that in a mirror she is always presented with the separateness of her features. Quite apart from the fact that they are individually large and sometimes plain, within the small circumference of her face, each part looks as though it has been put there by mistake and bears no relation to any of its fellow creatures.

The eyes are large and slightly protruding, as though she has an overactive thyroid. In fact, they are of an unusual brown, but their tendency to bulge, added to the fact that they watch behind gold-rimmed spectacles, give them an air of eager curiosity rather than attractiveness.

Her nose and mouth are in themselves inoffensive, even sensitive, being thin, straight and expressive. Sometimes when animated, her face takes on a curious alertness and intelligence, but in repose the effect, far from one of serenity, which she would have liked, hovers between emptiness and anxiety. Flickers of movement are apparent from each area of the face, uncoordinated and nervous. However, as soon as this image assails her, she rectifies it by smiling slightly and half shutting her eyes, which narrows them down to normal size, so that they match her mouth and nose.

Margot notices a small pink area on her chin and considers the possible causes for this. It could be that she is allergic to a new soap she has started to use, or that she is suffering from the nervous strain caused by Tony's rejected thesis, which he is in the process of revising.

Or perhaps she should not have applied that cheap make-up last night with that even cheaper cleansing cream. She would prefer to use better quality cosmetics, but instead goes for cut-price ones because of their low income. Besides, she is determined to throw off the shackles of an affluent American middle-class upbringing – all those expensive toys, clothes, gifts and trips her parents showered her with, topped off with the academically successful course at Vassar, where she majored in Sociology.

In fact, up to the age of eighteen, she was her parents' pride and joy, and she had managed to conceal from them her dissatisfaction with their mode of life. This demanded an enormous effort, since her feelings of rebellion had produced in her a disproportionate degree of hatred and resentment against them, as they represented the very system she was trying to reject.

Finally, while studying for her doctorate in England, she met Tony Harrison, several years younger than her; they had married while she was still in the middle of her course. Now, three years later, they are settled in Bridchester, a small, historic town in the East Riding of Yorkshire, not too far from

Hull University where Tony is simultaneously producing his thesis and lecturing at the university extension classes.

The lecturing has, in fact, gone extremely well, but for various reasons the thesis has been unsuccessful. Tony's enthusiasm for the subject waned after he wrote the first third of it, and his is the type of mind that requires a great deal of enthusiasm to inject vitality into his work. His approach tends to be intuitive and imaginative: he relies on inspiration, the almost visceral experience of re-living history, rather than distancing himself with a dry, analytical approach.

Margot has in some ways blamed herself for Tony's intellectual staleness. Recently she has been so occupied with their four-year-old daughter Hilary that she has not been able to summon up the time, energy and interest to maintain the mental rapport with him that previously sustained his enthusiasm.

But when she tentatively expressed this thought to Tony, he immediately scoffed at the idea and said that it was stretching the female conjugal role way beyond its normal sociological requirements. Margot had immediately laughed at his mockery of her academic jargon, and they dropped the subject.

She surveys the two plastic rubbish bins, placed next to each other in the cupboard under the sink. Taking one in each arm, she walks through the front garden of the flat to the alleyway, where four dustbins are stationed. As she upturns a heap of empty tins, cardboard boxes, paper bags, carrot peelings and rotten apples into the dustbin on the left, the problem of their finances needles away in her mind: until Tony has finished his thesis his lectures can only be minimal and despite the fact that she has taken on a full-time secretarial job, they are still finding that their social life demands considerable expenditure, and household frugality is therefore essential.

Two small boys peer over the fence at her from the next garden as she closes the dustbin lid.

'Hello,' Margot says.

'Hello,' the smaller boy replies. 'That's poisoned.'

'Really?' Margot never talks down to children, including her own daughter, so her instinct is to challenge him head on. 'No, of course it's not.'

'It is,' he insists.

She is about to reply, when it suddenly occurs to her that he might be in the middle of a detective story game, or simply indulging in a childish desire to shock and exaggerate. Either way, she is in no position to judge and maybe she shouldn't intrude upon his fantasy world – besides which, she is short of time.

'It's very, very poisonous,' the other boy says.

Margot laughs and returned to the kitchen. She peeps into the small bedroom at the back of the flat where Tony still lies sleeping. He is clutching the sheet over him and it has twisted round his body like a cocoon. The rest of the blankets and the eiderdown lie in a huddled heap on the floor, either by accident or design. Margot gently tries to flick the sheet round into its correct position, but Tony gives a grunt and wakes up as she does so.

'What time is it?' he mumbles.

'10.35. I'm just off to the launderette.'

'Exhausted,' he mutters and turning over, attempts to curl himself into a foetal position again, twisting the sheet round him into tight coils once more.

Margot sighs and collects up the laundry into a large polythene bag. She gains a curious satisfaction from dropping every possible item of clothing into it, whether the garment has only been worn once or has simply grown dusty from lying so long in the cupboard. She sometimes wonders whether her fastidious cleanliness has any psychological significance, but usually concludes that it is merely nice to be clean.

At the top of the bag she places a paperback and her purse. The launderette is twenty minutes' walk away. As she walks through Bridchester she encounters one or two of Tony's students whom she has met while waiting for him after his lectures. She feels slightly ashamed at her casual appearance, dressed as she is in faded blue jeans with a pale green shirt. The heavy laundry-bag reduces her gait to arrhythmical lurches.

In the launderette two Australian women are reading the Sunday papers. She listens inquisitively to their conversation as she piles her washing into one of the machines.

'There's an article in the supplement on sleep, Josie,' says a tall, suntanned woman with short, fair hair. 'I quote, "The amount of sleep one needs varies according to age, metabolism and the amount of energy expanded." You know, I don't think that's true at all, because I've completely changed. Two years ago, when I was twenty-four I used to sleep for hours. I needed at least ten hours a day, and over the weekend I could quite happily sleep till two. You should have seen my flatmate's face one day. She thought I was ill or something, but I wasn't. I just felt so lazy and relaxed—'

'You're really different now, Aileen.'

'Yes, I know. It's amazing, isn't it. I just can't stay in bed in the morning. So I mean, this article is rubbish because it's nothing to do with my metabolism—'

'Maybe it's affected by your age,' Josie suggests.

'Oh – two years? You must be joking. I'm not in my grave yet. Hey, I like that bag – where did you get it?'

'In Greece last year. It was fantastically cheap. The equivalent of about five shillings.'

'Oh, I must go to Greece,' Aileen says. 'I really must go on holiday soon. I'm sure I'm working too hard. Hey, do you know what Miss Bushnell was saying yesterday? You know, she's always up to something. Well, I thought something was brewing yesterday, because she and Paula were conferring for hours and then I had to type out a great big load of circulars about this new club they're forming.'

'What sort of club?'

'Oh, you know, local history and records and things, I think they're going to call it "The Bridchester Local History Society".'

Aileen's earnest attempt to say this in a posh English accent makes Josie laugh, and Margot, inserting coins into the machine, joins in.

Aileen turns and looks at her. 'Are you interested in it?' she says cordially.

'Well, I... I don't know. It just sounded kind of funny the way it came out like that.'

'Yes,' Aileen admits with a grin. 'Well, are you a student?'

'No, not really – I mean, no, not at all. My husband's doing his thesis – he's a historian, actually – and he does a bit of lecturing at the extension classes and, well, I just do secretarial work and typing in the daytime to pass the time.'

She doesn't say to pay the rent.

'Well, it's certainly one way of passing the time,' Aileen says, 'but hey, listen, are you interested in this club thing? They're very keen to get a few members to get it going.'

'What day does it meet?' asks Margot politely, but without much enthusiasm.

'Tuesday. We've got a few people interested in it already. Now what's the name of that scholar chappie, who's going to be the president? Mind you, he's never come to any of our meetings. They never do. Professor – Oh God, what's the name? … Newton or something.' Aileen screws up her face in her attempt to recall it.

'Not Professor Newsom?' asks Margot rhetorically.

'Could be something like that.'

'Is he a small man with a bald spot in the middle of his head – wears a hearing-aid?'

Aileen laughs. 'From that description I couldn't mistake him. Well, no, I don't know. I mean, I've never actually met the bloke. We just have to hear about him all day long. They're all so thrilled that he's agreed to participate. Apparently he's terribly busy and it's a great honour for us to have him.'

'Are you working for one of the faculties of the university or something?' asks Margot. Although irrepressibly curious, she always expressed it in a tentative manner, so it is never taken as rudeness.

'Oh no, it's the local Records Office, down in King Street. It's quite an interesting little place. You'd have expected them to have a local history society already, but apparently they did have one a few years ago and it petered out because of lack of interest.

'They were saying yesterday that everybody here was so busy and because there was so much on, nobody bothered to come along. But Miss Bushnell – she's the Head Archivist – has had this bee in her bonnet for some time that it's disgraceful not to have a local history society.

'Well, I think she wants to show off all our lovely manuscripts. At the moment they're mainly used by research students and historians and writers and other weird bods and she wants to make this wealth of knowledge available to the public – to broaden their minds and all that. So anyway, why don't you pop along one Tuesday? I think I've got a leaflet about it somewhere.'

Aileen pauses, slightly out of breath, and rummages in her bag for the circular, which she finally produces, creased and coffee-stained.

'Sorry it's such a mess. I was reading through some of them in my coffee break. Come to think of it, I might even join it myself. I may not be an academic, but it sounds rather fun.'

'Yes,' Josie says. 'Well, if you're living in a place, you feel you ought to know it's background.'

'Oh no. No good,' Aileen says. 'It's my art evening. Shame though.'

They each settle back to read their respective books and newspapers and as Margot watches the washing whirling round in yellow and green streaks, she thinks that it might be quite an informative activity and might even lift her out of the lethargy and dispiritedness she has lately been feeling.

3

Trouble at Round Table

ALISON Gregory walks briskly into the office.

'Paula, I have just discovered a student sharpening a pencil at the round table.'

'What?'

'Yes. It's a bit off, isn't it. I mean, it specifically says in the rules and regulations that it isn't allowed. I'm bloody furious.'

'What did you do?'

'Well, I told him where to go. He certainly won't be coming back here in a hurry.'

'Did you get his name?'

'Yes, I wrote it down in case he turned up again and we had any more trouble from him.'

She flicks over some papers in a file. 'Hugh Thomas.'

'Oh, I know him,' Paula Richards says. 'He isn't a bad bloke actually. He comes in quite often. Apparently he's a student at a local teacher's training college and he's doing a project on the Roman remains in Bridchester for his termly essay. He's really not that bad, and has never caused any trouble before. How funny that he should do a thing like that. I mean, he's quite bright. He must realise the harm that pencil sharpenings and lead dust can cause to some of the older manuscripts.'

'Well, he obviously hadn't read the rules properly.'

'Oh, I think we ought to give him another chance. He's terribly keen on this essay project, and it might get him into difficulties if he doesn't produce it. We can't ruin a man's career, can we?'

'Well, if he hasn't got the common sense to read the rules, he won't make much of a teacher,' Alison snaps, but then reads the *calm down* message in Paula's eyes. 'Oh well, I see your point. So shall I write a letter to him at the college telling him that he can use the secure room as long as he strictly observes the rules?'

'Yes, please,' says Paula, who is the Assistant Archivist, to Alison, who is her secretary.

'Actually, I felt a bit sorry for the bloke at the time,' Alison admits. 'God, he looked so sheepish when he saw me peering over his shoulder, just as he was blowing the dust off the desk. But I was so damn furious – I mean, how can people be so stupid? Haven't they any bloody sense? I don't know, the longer I work in this place, the more I seem to come into contact with idiots who don't use their minds.'

'Are you getting browned off again?' asks Paula, a note of concern in her voice.

'No, not especially, I mean, no more than usual. If only I could get my degree out of the way I'd probably be a bit more tolerant. I'm sure I must be hell to live with at the moment. I don't know how Steve puts up with it. Mind you, he's such an idiot, he deserves it.'

Alison works in the mornings only because – like Sandra Wilcox, the Records Office receptionist – she is studying part-time for an external degree in History. The course has taken four years part-time, and she is now in her final year, so naturally her nerves are overwrought.

'Oh dear,' she sighs. 'I'm one essay behind. I'm supposed to have handed it in yesterday. It's on the effects of the Industrial Revolution on France, but I haven't got down to it. I just never got a chance. Steve will keep inviting people over, just when I've arranged to work that evening. I don't know why the hell he does it. He just doesn't think.'

'Do you tell him when you intend to study?'

'Yes, of course I do, but he's so hopeless. He just forgets and invites people over all the same. I don't think he does it deliberately. Oh, well...'

She shrugs her shoulders and her words peter out.

Paula fetches two large volumes bound in red leather from the shelf behind her.

'I'm supposed to be calendaring that new collection presented by Sir John Dyson, but I haven't got round to it. I've got so much indexing to catch up with. Honestly, this place is so badly organised. Half the things we do could easily be done by clerical assistants, and then we'd have time to catch up on our professional duties. I think we could do with some O&M investigations—'

'Oh, Miss Bushnell would never hear of that,' Alison laughs. 'I mean, everything's been done in the same way for the past thirty-two years.'

'Is that how long she's been here?' Paula asks in surprise.

'Apparently – according to Bert anyway.'

Bert Goodrich is the records office caretaker and during his tenure has acquired vast stores of detailed information about the lives of the employees.

'It makes me sick how people can be like that,' Alison goes on. 'I mean, they always think they're right, just because they've been doing something for so long and it's impossible to communicate with them.'

'Well, it's not just her. I think she also finds it difficult to communicate with us, because she's of a different era and a different society.'

'OK, but who wants to communicate with her anyway?'

'Speaking of communication problems,' Paula says, 'I had a hilarious time last night watching Deirdre's tactics with Charles.'

According to Paula, her flatmate Deirdre has been conducting a low-profile but deeply felt love affair with her bachelor friend Charles for the past six years.

'How old is Deirdre?'

'Oh, she must be at least thirty-five, but she looks a lot older. She really doesn't make the best of herself. She could be quite nice looking if only she'd do something about her hair and her clothes and her figure. She looks so lumpy sometimes, all bundled up in tweed suits and cardigans. I'm sure, if only I had the guts to tell her, it might actually make Charles propose.'

'Well, why don't you?'

'I just can't bring myself to. It seems so unkind, though in fact it wouldn't be. It's partly the way she eats that makes her so fat. She's not one of those people who have a metabolic problem that makes them put on weight, but she eats nothing but starchy food – bread and cake and biscuits. For instance, this morning when I went into the kitchen to boil my egg, there was Deirdre, sitting at the table with a quarter pound of fruit cake on her plate. She was chopping up slice after slice and consuming it all, so what can you expect?'

'Perhaps you could send her an anonymous letter.'

'Oh, that wouldn't do any good. She'd be terrified out of her wits, poor thing, and would just grow paranoid, Perhaps I could use some subtle tactic like, "It's interesting how middle-aged men prefer skinny women," or "Did you notice Charles raving about Twiggy?"'

'Oh no, that would just reduce her to a state of despair. Perhaps you could just hide all her cake and biscuits or —'

'I know,' Paula says. 'You know, she's always catching on to new crazes. Well, I read of some food cult that requires one day's fasting a week. It's partly religious, because they feel it will make people appreciate the gift of food all the more for the other six days, and partly health – "internal cleanliness" and all that. Speaking of food, it's teatime, isn't it. Ah, talk of the devil.'

As Paula utters these words, Cynthia, the new office junior enters, bearing a tray with three cups of tea.

'Thank you,' Paula says, taking one for herself and one for Alison. 'Miss Bushnell is in the office upstairs. Would you mind taking it up to her?'

'No of course not,' Cynthia says, closing the door very quietly behind her.

'She looks very scared,' Paula says.

'Probably years of intimidation at home and at school. It's terrible what bullying can do to people. She can't be more than fifteen.'

'Oh, I expect she's got a ferocious mum or a dominating dad,'

'Well, I pity her if her bossy mum is anything like my mother-in-law.'

'Honestly, Alison, you sound like Les Dawson or Bernard Manning the way you go on about your mother-in-law.' And all delivered, Paula thinks but does not say, in the refined, cultivated voice Alison acquired at boarding school. The combination has an unusual impact.

'Well, she's so bloody possessive and interfering,' Alison replies, 'not only to Steve, which is bad enough, but even to me, which is infuriating. Last Sunday, when she came to tea, she started on about me having kids, and when I said I wasn't ready to have them yet – and I'm still not even sure if I want them at all – she nearly hit the roof. I mean, of all the cheek, to expect me to produce children just to please her. Oh well,' she sighs, 'I expect I'll turn into a childless, middle-aged neurotic with a passion for cats or felt toys or something.'

Paula laughs. 'At least your problems are material ones, like exams and whether to have children or not. Mine are so vague and insubstantial and—'

'Perhaps they're non-existent.'

'No, they certainly aren't. I mean, they do exist, but sometimes I feel I don't have any real problems.' Paula nibbles at a ginger biscuit she has found in a crumpled paper bag at the back of her desk drawer. 'There's just Douglas and our future is neatly planned out, and it's merely a question of being efficient and organising everything – you know, work, social life and even our emotions – so that nothing goes wrong and everything neatly fits together.

'And fifty per cent of the time I'm quite satisfied with that way of thinking. But then I get these awful, odd moments when... well, actually it came over me last Saturday, when I was at this party with Doug and I'd had too much to drink, but I felt I was seeing everything very clearly for the first time, and that everything was so superficial and that I wasn't really being myself and... oh, I don't know, I felt like I was searching for something.'

She sighs and they sit in pensive silence for a minute or two, sipping their tea. Alison has the ability to maintain a silence in the presence of her friends, which is in no way rude or even taciturn, but is highly communicative. She holds her cup between both hands, as though trying to work something out. Her large brown eyes gaze at Paula, whose long, curly hair, which is supposed to fall like a neat curtain, is ruffled with curls and ringlets and falls in untidy wisps around her shoulders.

'I know I'm being unreasonable,' Paula says at last.

'No you're not. It's just that... I mean, compared with a lot of people you're quite lucky. At least you do have a working relationship with him, and you've got a career and —'

'I know. It's funny to know simultaneously that one is asking for too much and to want it at the same time. But funnily enough, I think I'd chuck the career and the social life and the luxuries and the whole caboosh, if I could just feel that I'd found... I don't know whatever it is I'm looking for. I'm settled, but at the same time I'm drifting...'

Alison's face suddenly changes and her upper lip curls into a mocking, disdainful smile. 'What you need, Paula, is some nice, quiet hobby to interest you. Take the Bridchester Local History Society, for instance.'

'Oh don't,' Paula says. 'If I hear another word about that wretched club, I'll scream. Poor old Miss B thinks she's redeemed the whole university down the road at Hull, not to mention Bridchester itself, by its formation. She's been in a very good mood for the last three weeks.'

'How did she think up the idea?' asks Alison.

'Well, apparently a friend of Professor Newsom's, who's a local doctor, wanted to track down some obscure piece of information about a title deed to a piece of land he owns. He came to the Records Office and was highly impressed.' Paula mimics the scholarly middle-class tone of Newsom's friend.

'I should bloody well hope so,' laughs Alison, 'after all the sweat and tears we put in.'

'And he suggested to Humphrey—'

'Who the hell's Humphey?'

'Humphrey, my dear, happens to be Professor Newsom. It suits him rather well, I think. Anyway, he told Humphrey that it was a pity that the local townspeople didn't get more information about our wretched archives etcetera. So of course Humphrey rushed straight round to Maggie—'

'Maggie?' Alison interrupts again.

'Margaret—'

'Oh Miss Bushnell.'

'Yes, straight round to Margaret, absolutely burning with the idea.'

Alison snorts and then coughs, as her tea goes down the wrong way. 'God, can't you just imagine it. Those two having scholastic confabs with polysyllabic pronouncements.'

'It sounds rather like an ancient Druid rite, the idea of them exchanging profundities. What's more, they've had not merely one meeting, but dozens of them. Miss Bushnell was in a state over it for days.'

'Yes, I noticed she's started wearing clothes she imagines are more fashionable – mainly floral creations – over the past few weeks,' Alison happily joins in the bitching.

'Well, apparently they did the trick, because despite the fact that Newsom is "overburdened with work", to quote her, he's done an enormous amount of organising for the society and has raked in loads of old dears who are interested in joining.'

'Mmm,' Alison's eyes glint with amusement, 'shall we go along for a laugh?'

'What?'

'Oh, go on. It sounds terrific. I'd love to see what happens when it gets going. It'll be an absolute scream, with Margaret casting coy glances at Humphrey over the Dundee cake, and everyone in ecstasies about the discovery of some ancient memorial roll.'

'Well, I get enough of that at work,' Paula says caustically. 'I'm always terrified of becoming an archives bore, That's why I deliberately try to steer clear of it out of working hours.'

'I don't see how you can very well steer clear of this. I mean you're so completely involved in this office that they'll automatically expect you to turn up.'

'Yes and that's exactly what I object to. It's this feeling that because you're employed as something, you're at your firm's beck and call at all hours, in and out of work. Well, I'm not going to be pushed around —'

'No, Paula, don't be a spoil-sport.' Alison stands up and walks over to the window. Her long legs emerge from a skimpy yellow miniskirt, giving her the appearance of an overgrown buttercup.

'Oh do come,' she repeats. 'Well, I'm going anyway, just for a laugh, and I've got to have someone to share my catty jokes with. I mean, it's no fun being bitchy about people all on one's own.'

The truth of this cannot be denied. 'Yes, I see what you

mean,' Paula says. 'Well, I'll come then, but I'm jolly well not going to start working fingers to the bone for the society, which I'm sure is what they'll all expect me to do.'

'Who's "they"? You're beginning to sound rather paranoid,' Alison jokes.

'Oh, you know what I mean. I suppose basically I'm afraid it will ruin my social life. I mean, you know how time-consuming those clubs can be, and if you get landed with being the secretary or treasurer, you simply have no time left to call your own.'

They lapse into silence and Alison returns to her typing, while Paula flicks over the pages of an old bibliography. The bottom half of one page has been torn out, which annoyingly enough contains the item she wanted to check. She makes a note in her diary to consult the reference copy in the central library.

The sun shines in through the long windows, which run the length of the wall on the left, and casts deep shadows onto the books. Paula soon grows absorbed in indexing, her mind stimulated by the complexity of the work; her emotional uncertainties lulled into obeisance by the hypnotic rhythm of Alison's typing.

4

Dana

AS DANA Newsom walks down the slope leading to the hospital doorway, she realises with annoyance that the throbbing in her wrist has not disappeared and that after three weeks of muddled visits to her GP, the visit to the specialist is likely to be ineffective. Her life always seems unpredictable and disorganised, and this inopportuneness she bears with wry resignation, verging at times on cynicism, though it sometimes leads to fitful outbursts of bad temper.

The hospital interior smells of new paint and antiseptic, The receptionist tells her that the outpatients department is in the basement and as usual she takes the wrong staircase so that she finds herself wandering through a labyrinth of kitchens. She neatly dodges from side to side to avoid a series of cooks slowly wheeling heavy metal trolleys down the passages. The antiseptic smell has by now been replaced by a rather unpleasant odour of stew mingled with cabbage and onions.

At last, twisting through several small turnings with sloping linoleum floors, she manages to locate the outpatients department, and registers at the reception desk to find there is a particularly long queue of people to be seen before her.

'It's very heavy this morning, dear,' says the receptionist.

Dana's mind immediately conjures up an image of a

stone-grey sky, laden with black clouds.

'Poor Dr Mueller is absolutely inundated.'

Dana sits down and takes out of her bag a paperback edition of Thomas Mann short stories. She starts to read, but her concentration, never very good at the best of times, and particularly shaky in the morning, is soon diverted by the dialogue between two middle-aged ladies sitting to her right.

'My dear, he's got such a beautiful accent. It really amazes me, because he can't have been in England all that long.'

'Oh, they all have,' her friend replies. 'I mean, that sort of person has been to university in Heidelberg or one of those places and of course they learn to speak the most beautiful English.'

'Well, exactly. In fact, he's got a perfect Oxford accent. And it's really amazing, when you think of it.'

Dana's attention wanders at this stage and drifts to the forces of intellectual snobbery she has noticed around her since her arrival in Hull six months previously. Despite the fact that she is Professor Newsom's daughter, she has been brought up and educated in Ontario, the home of her divorced mother and Dana's return to her father's native land is not the result of filial duty but simply an accident. After dropping out of college in the middle of her second year, she met Mike, an English journalist visiting Ontario at the time, and accompanied him back to Hull; they now live in Bridchester a few miles away.

Dana's lack of occupation does not bother her, though it occasionally worries Mike and greatly worries her father. She is content 'to live creatively', as she calls it, concocting elaborate new recipes, making paper flowers and collages, and producing batique scarves. She has recently joined a pewter-work class at Bridchester School of Arts & Crafts, and has become so immersed in the peripheral activities of this college that she has little time left to reflect on her lack of paid occupation.

Occasionally when bills arrive and Mike becomes conscious of their financial problems, they will have a brief, bitter, sometimes violent quarrel about what he terms her laziness and what she terms her creative fulfilment. In the end, however, it is always Dana who wins, by her silences and tears and displays of hidden sensitivity, the depth of which he has not previously been aware, and a reconciliation will take place, to be followed by a particularly elaborate dinner, and an abundance of new scarves.

Dana is above all things honest with herself. She considers dishonesty to oneself to be worse than dishonesty to others and maintains with strict discipline an inner integrity which prohibits hypocrisy, delusion or superficiality. Snobbery in any of its forms is abhorrent to her, and a certain brand of intellectual snobbery, which has recently come to her notice, has been not only offensive but even intolerable to her. She is on the verge of asking the woman next to her what is so marvellous about an Oxford accent as opposed to any other accent, when her name is called out by the nurse.

She is led into the cubicle next door to wait her turn.

'Ah, Nancy Newsom,' the nurse says jokingly, reading her name off her file. Dana thinks how pathetic the pun on her name is, but forces a watery smile and tries to get back to her Thomas Mann.

As she sits there waiting, she thinks how odd it is to be at a point in one's life where something is about to be decided, and not to know what the decision is. Dana is in no way a hypochondriac and is not even particularly concerned about her wrist. It is merely the implications of the moment that catch her interest.

She feels some kind of duty to think or act in a particular way at such a moment, as though by an exertion of the will a certain effect may be achieved, and immediately dismisses the thought as neurotic and illogical. She has a healthy contempt for neurosis and illogicality, which she is, in fact, called upon to invoke on many occasions, since her temperament and circumstances are such that traits of neurosis and illogicality often emerge in her mind. She feels she possesses an unusual clarity of mind at this moment, a blend of relaxation and alertness that is so difficult to achieve and which, she feels, could only be attained by chance. Thinking this, her mood instantly dissolves and she is left bored and restless.

She glances at a blue leaflet pinned to the notice-board on the wall behind her and issued by the Bridchester Local History Society. As she scans it, she sees with amusement her father's name in prominent black capitals. It is typical of him to get roped in to such an 'establishment' enterprise.

Although Dana scorns inter-family dependence, and family life as such, she cannot with a clear conscience absent herself from such a meeting, where her father's scholastic pretensions, as she considers them to be, will once again exhibit themselves in organised pageantry, but where her attendance is nevertheless called for by her own moral code of behaviour.

5

June

JUNE Brentwood deftly whips up a meal for her husband's supper from an assortment of tins and packets of frozen food. By the time Tom arrives home twenty minutes later, the table is laid, the food cooked and music is blaring from the portable Japanese radio lurking behind a plantpot of chives.

'Goodness, what a racket!' he says, flinging his jacket over a chair. June stretches out her left hand while carrying on whisking a white sauce with her right hand, and switches off the radio.

'Sorry,' she says, 'I needed something to calm my shattered nerves.'

'Have the brats been their usual sweet selves?' he asks, sitting down and putting his feet up on the top rung of the kitchen steps.

'Yes, the little darlings, I could strangle them,' June says, sprinkling white pepper onto the sauce.

'Hey, that's enough. You don't want to choke us, do you? So what were they up to today?'

'What weren't they up to,' June gives an exasperated sigh as she stirs the sauce. 'Three of them had accidents, two fell over and cut their knees, one of them was bullying a new West Indian kid. I hate to see racial prejudice in children. Another one actually — '

'Look, June,' Tom says, picking up the evening paper, 'I really think you'll have to give up this job if it's getting you down.'

'No, it's not getting me down,' she replies with an artificial, high, tinkling laugh. 'It's all terrific fun actually.'

'Oh sure.' He turns to the Arts page.

'I mean, just because I haven't got any sense of vocation — '

'There's a difference between having no sense of vocation and hating children as much as you do.'

June winces. 'Now Tom, that's not fair. I don't "hate" children and you know I don't. Otherwise, I would never have taken this job. It's just that I'm not terrible keen on them.'

'Same thing.'

'No, it's not. And anyway, I'm sure I'd love my own.'

'Oh my God. There's no need to try and mollify me. I'm not arguing with you and I'm not telling you off. I'm on your side. I just think you'd be better off doing something else – and so would the children.'

'Why should they do something else?' asks June stupidly.

'No, I mean they would be better off if you were doing something else.'

She pours the sauce over his fish and hands him a portion of it on a pink plate. 'Help yourself to vegetables,' she says.

'Thanks. This looks most creative. No, I mean, there are lots of things you could do.'

'No, there aren't.' Jane raises her voice. 'Having a degree in History is totally useless jobwise, unless you've got some other qualification or you're particularly brilliant in your subject field, which I'm not. Oh, this is ridiculous. We've been over this so many times.'

'Well, you don't have to go out to work. There's no financial necessity.'

'Yes, obviously, but it's a help. Anyway, I just couldn't sit at home twiddling my thumbs all day long. I'd get so bored. I'm so restless.'

Tom sighs. 'There must be something you could do. Couldn't you get some administrative job or local government work or something?'

'Yes, I could. But it would be boring.'

'My dear June—'

'Don't you dare "my dear" me,' she laughs. 'And you can switch off your lecturer's voice for a start.'

'My dear June,' Tom ignores her, 'most jobs are boring, and since you haven't any other qualifications, I think you'd better reconcile yourself to having a boring job. Actually, I don't see why you don't do a secretarial course. At least being a private secretary or a personal assistant would offer more mental stimulation.'

'Actually I don't think any of them are boring. It's just me. I haven't the facility for making jobs interesting.'

'There's no need for all this self-deprecation. You're lively and intelligent and very creative. You just don't happen to have found your metier yet.'

'Actually, I agree with you. I think I ought to do a secretarial course. It's just that I've been too lazy to get down to it. Now I wonder where I could go for it...'

Tom runs his hands through his hair. 'Well, I should think the Poly is best. It's just off Church Lane—'

'Oh, I know where it is. I'll go and get some details from

tomorrow.'

She picks up the oven-cloth and removes a glass baking dish of stewed apple, which she places on the table.

'I don't think you've been going out enough,' he says.

'You're right. I'm in danger of turning into a dreary suburban housewife.'

Tom laughs. 'No danger of that.'

'Well, I could do with going out a bit more. I tend to feel like a grass widow when you're lecturing in the evenings.'

'Yes, I really must try and get the times changed.' He rests his chin on his hand.

'Oh, don't be silly. I don't want you to have to start contorting your timetable and ruining your career because of me. No, the best idea is for me to join a few clubs and meet a few other "lecture widows".'

'Well, you could join a choir and—

'Yes, I could. I like singing, though my sight-reading isn't very good and—'

'Hey, hang on. I've had an idea. Something cropped up when I was at the Records Office tonight. Now where did I put that leaflet? Oh, it must be... ah, here it is.'

He fishes a blue leaflet out of his briefcase and hands it to her.

'This looks interesting,' June says, reading through it.

'I've never actually been to Bridchester Records Office before and I've always been meaning to go. I expect there'll be some funny old dears at this group, but the subject looks fascinating.'

'Bridchester five thousand years ago, and there are some interesting excursions,' June says. 'Oh, this is really me.'

Tom laughs. 'Well, it'll give you something to think about

51

instead of wasting all your emotional energy fuming about the kids at school. By the way, you may as well hand in your notice at the end of the week. I really think it's the best thing. You were only on supply anyway, and I understand they've got a huge list of willing teachers to fill the post.'

'I know, and I will, but I still feel guilty – partly because I've failed at the job, and also because I feel I ought to like children more than I do.'

Tom clicks his tongue in annoyance. 'If you don't watch out, you're going to develop an obsession about your so-called dislike of children. Just forget about it, and presumably you'll start to like them again once you're out of a pressure situation with them. But I certainly think you ought to start going out a bit more. You're getting too self-absorbed.'

6

Alison

A STREAM of people file slowly out of the bus as Alison attempts to flatten herself in front of the window of the furniture shop. It is 1.25 pm and her husband Steve Gregory is late as usual for his lunch appointment with her.

She resolves to wait another ten minutes, and then go back to the office and eat some sandwiches. She can never bear to spend money on lunch in a restaurant by herself – it always makes her feel immoral, as she once explained to Paula.

She looks at her watch in irritation. It really is impossible the way Steve is continually either forgetting to arrive or arriving half an hour late. His lack of organisation exasperates her, more particularly because it is not the result of any cognitive defect, such as stupidity or bad memory, but rather because of his nonchalant attitude, which verges on apathy and indifference.

She has been particularly looking forward to lunch with him this morning as it is a fresh spring day and she has planned to go to the new open-air French bistro round the corner. She watches a woman walk by in a brown suede pinafore dress, which looks far too hot for this weather. It is amazing, she thinks, the unsuitable clothes people wear. It requires so little ingenuity to assemble a suitable outfit. She does not object to unconventional clothes, but rather to these incongruous concoctions, lacking in style, which are neither one thing or another.

A tall Chinese man, in brick-red shirt and dark-rimmed spectacles, walks up the road in one direction and re-emerges in the opposite direction armed with a smaller, younger Chinese man. This incident reminds her of a child's picture-puzzle, where you form a group of people by manipulating the pieces, or narrow down the group by a process of elimination.

Alison is often amused by totally factual events that appear incongruous or ridiculous to her. She smiles as this thought strikes her, and a passing soldier, assuming the smile is intended for him, smile back at her. Alison blushes and twists round awkwardly, beginning to feel annoyed.

The irritating factor is not knowing why Steve has not arrived. It is worrying to be left in ignorance about something, however trivial. It could be because he has been delayed at the office or because he has had to cancel lunch, or even because he has not gone to work at all today, having been afflicted with one of his frequent bouts of hypochondria.

She sighs in irritation. It is so difficult for her to accept people for what they are. She always feels the need to criticise them and, in her imagination, to improve them, just as she feels the desire to dress people in clothes that would suit them better and to furnish their houses in new styles. A mixture of perfectionism and restlessness is so totally ingrained in her character that she makes no attempt to rectify it, but regards it as her 'critical abilities'.

Eventually Steve arrives, panting and dishevelled, and insists on going to a Greek restaurant, which he says is just up the road, but which turns out to be a good ten minutes' walk away. As they sit down, Alison looks at her watch and sees that it is 1.40 pm.

'I'll have to gulp this down,' she says. 'I've got a lecture at 2.15.'

'Oh, don't be so neurotic,' Steve replies.

Alison is furious. 'I'm not being neurotic. I just happen to be a few degrees more efficient than you are, which isn't saying much. I must say your excuses for being late grow weirder every time. An old school friend indeed! You just bloody forgot.'

Steve turns pale with indignation. 'Give it a rest, Alison. Stop speaking to me as though I'm a school kid.'

Alison, growing more irritable every moment, a combination of enervation and hunger, slams her purse down on the table and hands him a pound note. 'For God's sake, eat your bloody dinner by yourself. I'm leaving you the money for it because you're so hopeless you've probably forgotten to bring your wallet with you.'

She stands up angrily and is about to leave when a waiter appears. He is a short, thickset man with mobile lips and expressive eyes, which are busily attempting to placate the couple at this particular moment.

'I'm very sorry, sir. No *dolmades* left. No *kioftedes* either. Only English dishes.'

Alison bursts out laughing and sits down again.

'Oh goodness, this is too much,' she says. 'What a life.'

They order an English lunch and resume their normal tone of conversation – a mixture of verbal combat and guarded friendliness.

7

Paula

PAULA is seated next to Douglas in the third row of the concert hall, stiffly holding the programme between them. It is in three parts: first Bach, Mozart and Beethoven – all well-known pieces – played by the Bridchester Symphony Orchestra, followed by an interval; then some new musical arrangements of Shakespeare songs, to be performed by a local soprano; and finally after a second interval the evening is to be rounded off with Elgar's Cello Concerto.

Douglas Gifford has been particularly uncommunicative this evening, sitting bolt upright and occasionally twitching. He is worried about the backlog of work that has piled up in his office during his holiday in Crete the previous fortnight with two friends, and Paula has the distinct impression that his enjoyment of the holiday has made the daily routine of his life as a chartered accountant pall in comparison. Since his return he had been morose, curt and taciturn.

'We can't stay for coffee after the concert,' he tells her during the first interval. 'I must have an early night as I'll need to get into work an hour earlier, we're so loaded up.'

Paula laughs and makes the worst possible response in the circumstances.

'The office won't fall down if you're not there at the crack of dawn.'

Douglas twitches and, lifting his handkerchief from his breast pocket, wipes his hands, which are damp with perspiration.

'You obviously have no idea of the way the industry is run. We're not some piffling, arty concern. And there's no point in taking that sarcastic tone. You know the sort of person I am and I can't change.'

Paula immediately feels remorseful because of the reasonableness of his argument. though amused at his snide reference to the records office.

'Sorry, Douglas,' she says. 'Oh look, she's going to sing the three songs from *Hamlet*. I had to sing 'Tomorrow Is St Valentine's Day' for a concert when I was in the guides.'

Douglas laughs. 'How ghastly. I can imagine a troupe of gangly girl guides warbling enthusiastically. Fortunately I was never in the scouts, but if I had been I'd have probably been roped in for a similar function. I had quite a good mezzo soprano at the age of nine.'

Paula giggles. Doug can be fun when he forgets his near perpetual worries about perfection at work and status-seeking in society.

'I remember we had a whole group of aunts and cousins down to stay with us in the country one summer,' he recalls. 'We were an enormous group, revoltingly gregarious, and every evening we used to put on shows. One evening I was just in the middle—'

'Ssshhh...' says a voice behind them and looking up, Paula sees that the soprano has walked on to the stage – a large woman in an elaborate and cumbersome purple satin dress. Paula waits expectantly for Douglas's predictable whisper.

'Much too heavy. Why do they always try and dress up in the period. It never comes off,' he breathes into her right ear.

They listen absorbed until the second interval, during which Douglas gives Paula a series of concise opinions, most of them negative, on the soprano's performance.

'I think her grace notes were slightly slurred. It's a very fine point, and difficult to pin down, because she does them so fast, but it jangles on my nerves.'

Paula is thinking to herself wryly that it does not take much to jangle Douglas's nerves, when she sees Margaret Bushnell approaching them from the front of the hall, accompanied by a tall woman in a rather too long beige coat with a matching beige hat.

'Good evening,' Miss Bushnell says, obviously delighted by the joke that they, who are accustomed to meeting within the work confines of the Records Office, should actually be meeting outside it. 'What a surprise to see you here.'

Paula politely introduces her to Douglas, and Miss Bushnell in turn introduces her friend, Mrs Angela Withers-Browne.

'Look, why don't we meet for coffee after the concert,' Margaret suggests cordially. 'I'm sure Angela would be most interested to hear from you the inside story about our work. I mean, I always feel that in my administrative capacity, I'm not in a true position to describe our work in the same detail as one of my subordinates.'

Paula notes the slight emphasis on the word 'subordinates' and feels doubly embarrassed, both at the fact that Douglas does not want to stay up late this evening, and at the prospect of the efforts she will now have to make to establish a social relationship with her employer. However, she smiles politely and says, 'How kind of you, Miss Bushnell. Thank you so much, we'd love to.'

Margaret and Angela return to their seats and Paula is left to bear the brunt of Douglas's indignation.

'Are you absolutely scatterbrained, or are you deliberately trying to sabotage me,' he explodes, insofar as he can explode in a subdued whisper.

'I'm sorry, Douglas, but I simply can't ruin my career in one night.'

'Oh, how can it be that important to have coffee with the old bag—'

'Yes, it is. You don't understand. She's terribly sensitive and terribly easily offended. She'd definitely take it personally if I refused. I'm sorry, truly I am, Douglas, but I really couldn't say no.'

Douglas lapses into a sullen silence, which is soon interrupted by the appearance on stage of the female cellist, who is about to tackle the Elgar.

'Good God,' he mutters, gazing with disbelief at her low-cut orange taffeta gown. 'That takes a lot of beating.'

8

Inauguration

MARGARET Bushnell stands on the steps of the town hall, waiting to greet the guests to the reception buffet held in honour of the inauguration of the Bridchester Local History Society. She is dressed, as Alison predicted to Paula yesterday, in her best pink lamé suit, her hair freshly permed with a blue rinse, and a note of merriness in her voice to mask her anxiety as she greets each guest individually, ticking off their names from the list of new members.

While her back is turned, engaged in a long conversation with one of the deans at Hull University on the parking problems in the vicinity, Dana Newsom and her partner Michael Brennan slip in uninvited. Because of Dana's lack of organisation she has neglected to enrol for the club in time, but they have turned up nevertheless, determined to hear Professor Newsom's opening speech.

'God, I've never seen so many people in this room before,' she whispers to Mike.

They make their way through the assembly room, which is decorated in a variety of unmatching greens, from olive-green curtains, to lime-green window frames and grass-green carpet, with rows of tenebrous oil paintings lining the walls.

'I wonder who thought up the colour scheme,' she says.

'It must have taken a genius to produce this effect of visual cacophony,' Mike replies. He is given to uttering slick phrases, which he will afterwards recall and use in his articles. 'I wonder if anyone's reporting this do.'

'It's not particularly significant,' Dana says disparagingly, 'but it will probably make the *Bridchester Gazette*.'

She wanders towards the trestle tables, covered in white cloths, and helps herself to a large slice of squashy chocolate cake, topped with whipped cream. Just as she is about to take her first bite, she notices a woman in a pink lamé suit approaching her like a guided missile honing in on its target.

'Excuse me,' she says to Dana. 'You weren't invited to this function. I didn't tick your name off on the list.'

Dana is not acquainted with Margaret Bushnell and is therefore unfamiliar with her phenomenal memory for names and faces, nor with her particular brand of rudeness. She can only stare at her open-mouthed, torn between anger, amazement and frustrated hunger as the Head Archivist of the Records Office walks off, spectacles glinting brightly under the myriad lights that hang from long chains from the ceiling.

'Good God,' Dana explodes to Mike, as she takes a big, comforting bite of the chocolate cake. 'Did you ever see such rudeness? What absolute cheek!'

'Oh, she's quite a character,' he laughs. 'Don't worry, it's only her way of speaking.'

'*Her way of speaking?* You must be joking!'

'Well, she's an efficient old thing and she was perfectly right – we *weren't* invited,' he says in a soothing, reasonable tone.

'What do you mean, we weren't invited?' Dana says furiously. 'I just saw the notice up somewhere about the reception and it didn't mention anything about invitations or subscribing to the club or anything. I mean, if they don't make these things clear, what can they expect? Well, she's got a hell of a nerve. I simply can't get over it. I mean, you don't expect to find that sort of behaviour in a grown woman.'

'Oh calm down. Anyway, now we're here we might as well make the most of it.'

'Well, I can't for a start,' Dana says petulantly, finishing off the chocolate cake and wiping her lips with a paper napkin. 'She's completely taken away my appetite. What a bloody nerve!'

'I say!' exclaims a tall woman, with her hair piled up in a bun, and dressed in a combination of greys. 'Have you just had a row with Miss Bushnell?'

'Well, I don't know what her name was. Some woman in ghastly pink and she was damned rude to us.'

'Oh don't worry, it's not you. She's in a foul temper. I work at the Records Office and I've just been told that everything's gone wrong.'

'Don't exaggerate, Alison,' says the man she is with, who is the same height as her, possibly an inch taller, but somehow gives the impression of being slightly shorter, perhaps because he seems so relaxed and laid back.

'Oh well, maybe you're right Steve,' she says. 'There's not that much that can go wrong at one of these dos... It's a dreadful place to have it in though.'

'Yes,' Dana laughs, 'we were just commenting on the hideousness of the colour scheme.'

'It's incredible, isn't it,' Alison says. 'I mean, you couldn't even describe to anyone just how lurid it is.'

'Yes, you have to see it to savour its impact,' Dana says. 'I was told by—'

'Ssshhh...' come a chorus of voices, and Dana looks up to hear someone thumping on the table at the far end of the hall.

Everyone stands up to get a better view of the proceedings. Margaret Bushnell is standing at the right end of the table; in the middle sits Professor Newsom; and Paula is on the left.

'It it my very pleasant duty,' rings out the crisp, soprano tones of Miss Bushnell, 'to welcome you all today to the inaugural meeting of our newly formed association.'

Dana giggles quietly and whispers, 'What association?' provocatively in Mike's ear.

'For some time many of us have felt that there was something missing in the community of Bridchester. We are bound together by many things, by the local churches in this area, by the university in Hull, by our sports teams—' she smiles '— though as an ignorant member of the fair sex I know very little about these athletic matters...'

Everybody laughs politely.

'From the university spring many offshoots – extension classes, clubs, societies, numerous activities, and I am sure that the community as a whole feels bound together by the daily contact with the students.

'But one factor of our little town that has so far been overlooked is its wonderful history and the wealth of historical artefacts, both in the physical evidence of five thousand years and in the written record – and, as many of you will know, the Records Office of which I am proud to be the Head Archivist, is in possession of an archive going back many centuries.

'It is not by accident, therefore, that we have here today

some of the most notable historians and lecturers in History that our community and the university can boast of – or should I say—' she smiles again '—of whom our community and the university can boast. In the excitement of the occasion, I fear my grammar has gone haywire.'

Everybody laughs politely again, though this time a little wearily.

'For indeed, it has been an exciting enterprise for myself and for all the members of my staff.'

She smiles again, this time meaningfully across the table at Paula, who sits diminutive and pale, at the other end of the table, clearly nervous and ill at ease.

'However, I will not bore you with the many details of the preparations and organisational meetings that have led to the formation of this society. Suffice it to say that we have come into being, and I hope and indeed believe that this society will grow to be a creative enterprise, and one worthy of the scholastic reputation of Bridchester – and of course our big brother, Hull.'

There is a ripple of applause, which increases to a crescendo as she sits down, and then there is a very long pause before anything else happens.

She stands up again laughing. 'I'm so sorry, I completely forgot to say a few words about Professor Newsom, who is to deliver our inaugural lecture on Bridchester five thousand years ago. As you know, Professor Humphrey...'

It is at this point that Dana takes Mike's arm and drags him out of the hall, pushing aggressively through groups of people who are standing with polite, frozen smiles, which change to irritation as Dana resolutely makes her way in a straight line towards the exit and out of the door.

'What on earth's the matter with you?' asks Mike when they are out of earshot. 'I thought you wanted to hear your father's speech.'

'I know. I did. I'm sorry. Truly I am, but I simply couldn't stand it any more.'

'Stand what?' asks Mike in irritation, anticipating correctly one of Dana's moods of rebellion against the establishment.

'Oh, the whole set-up. The pomposity and hypocrisy and formality. The whole darned artificiality of it all, It makes me sorry to know that my father is caught up in this sort of life and—'

'Oh, there's no need for such puerile histrionics, Dana.' Mike makes a mental note of the phrase 'puerile histrionics'. 'What can you expect if you go to a formal occasion?' he continues. 'There's nothing evil about formality. Admittedly it can be irritating, time-consuming, even downright boring, but there's no need to make a moral issue out of it.'

'But there is, Mike. Don't you see? It's because you've been brought up to all this that you can't shake it off. It's bred in the bone and you don't seem to realise it.'

'Realise what?' asks Mike, taking her by the arm and leading her out of the town hall into the grey street outside.

'Your dependence on convention. You're terrified to do anything that provokes criticism or notice or comment. I mean, when I protested about the ridiculousness of the meeting and made my exit, and moved through all those people, you looked positively embarrassed – no, more than embarrassed, you looked ashamed. And yet, there's nothing to be ashamed of. We're living in an age when we each have the independence and the right to make our opinions felt, to pro-

65

test against things when we disagree with them. All this cow-towing to others, because they're older and more established, just makes me want to puke.'

Mike knows that there is no point in trying to argue with Dana. He agrees with some of her ideas, but not all of them. Moreover, her eyes are not arguable with at the best of times, and even more particularly so on this occasion, when she is obviously out of temper because of Margaret Bushnell's snub.

She lapses into silence and they walk arm in arm down the road, achieving, as Mike considers, a better communication in silence than they do by talking, and the evening darkness slowly descends on the quiet side streets of Bridchester, so that by the time they have reached their flat, their garden is obscured in shadows of grey and dark green.

9

Asperges

MARGOT listens to the church bells ringing slowly and rhythmically as the Asperges are sung. The music is so fluent that it makes her think of drops of blood falling onto the snow and then melting into pink pools.

The smell of incense drifts towards her, strong, pure and cleansing. Pinpoints of candlelight flicker on all sides and the richness of the primary colours of the stained-glass windows is emphasised by the contrasting shadows in the corners of the church.

Margot has decided to attend High Mass following a moment of insight when she was pegging sheets to the washing line at seven o'clock this morning. She always gets up early on Sundays to get through the ever-higher mass of household chores that her perfectionist nature dictates she needs to complete before she can participate more fully in Tony's social and intellectual activities once the work is out of the way.

While she was hanging up the washing she noticed the dew gleaming in green reflected drops on the longer grasses and as she listened to the slow murmur of the distant traffic, she suddenly felt a moment of inner peace – or had it been the wonder of nature? – which seemed to have been evoked by the contrast between the natural scenery and the dull steady background dirge of the industrialised world.

At that moment Margot felt at one with her surroundings. The mood passed quickly, and as always, she regretted her inability to sustain such inner states of serenity, but valued them for the brief seconds of their duration, and would try to recapture them afterwards. But on this occasion the attempt had proved unsuccessful. She was seized with a vivid memory of herself in adolescence, when she was often possessed by such moods until they had disappeared with her loss of faith at the age of nineteen.

In respect for the person she had been, she had felt a longing to go to High Mass, perhaps in the hope of renewing her faith. In fact, the aesthetic pleasure that Margot always used to experience at Mass remains undiminished, but the flashes of insight and wonder, which in her teens had illuminated this, have now proved to be far less than she had imagined.

Tony once said that he could only be moved to belief by an intensely appreciative experience of a piece of music or a work of art, and at the time she had dismissed this idea because her own beliefs had been inspired by an awareness of joy and suffering, and of other human beings, and she had felt that faith should not be an offshoot of aestheticism.

Yet while she is listening to the Asperges she grasps what Tony meant, for the complete visual and aural harmony that engulfs her bring a peace that is paradoxically ecstatic. The purity of the voices seems to transcend vowels and consonants, so that the vowels are open and the consonants are inconspicuous, to allow the music to emerge more freely.

Margot's thoughts during the rest of the Mass are concentrated on following the service and afterwards, as she joins the group for coffee in the church hall, she feels a mixture of wonder and emptiness, wonder at the mystery that has revealed itself to her, but emptiness in not fully committing herself as she once had, for nowadays the intellectual habit of questioning and criticism has worn away at any belief she once had.

As she sits down at a long wooden table to drink her coffee she notices a very thin woman in a duffle coat, with long black hair and on odd, bony face, whose features, like hers, seem uncoordinated, only more so. The woman sits nervously, twisting her hands together and then suddenly grasping her cup and gulping down her coffee, she springs up and approaches a priest with a white stick, whom she leads back to the table.

'Father Peter,' she says, 'I can't agree that we are God's friends. We are His people, because He made us, but we are not His friends.'

'I disagree with you there, Anna,' the priest replies, his eyes unfocussed and screwed up, the small black pupils slightly awry. 'He made us, so we are His people, but we are also His friends and—'

'Excuse me, Father Peter,' interrupts a well-built young man with a shock of yellow hair, 'could you possibly have a word with Father John, he's been looking for you.'

'Of course,' Father Peter replies, and the young man escorts him across to the other side of the hall.

Anna sits down opposite Margot. She looks down at the table and fidgets with her coffee spoon before suddenly looking up and darting a piercing look at Margot.

'Do you believe that we are God's people?'

'I don't really know,' Margot says, slightly taken aback, and then, responding to her openness, adds, 'I'm afraid I haven't thought about religion for a long time. I feel very bad about it, actually.'

'Oh, I wasn't trying to make you feel guilty or anything.'

'Oh no, I know you weren't,' Margot replies.

A tall woman in a navy coat approaches and Margot realises that she is a nurse.

'Anna,' she says, 'we must be getting back.'

'Oh,' Anna pouts. 'I wanted to stay and talk.'

'I'm sorry, dear, but you know we really haven't got time. We've got to be back for lunch.'

Margot wonders how old Anna is: she could be anything between sixteen and forty.

'Oh.' For a moment Anna's face puckers up slightly, as though she is going to cry, and then she changes her mind and, with a stony stare at the nurse, replies, 'Well, if you say I'll have to go, I'll have to, won't I. I mean, it's not for me to make judgments.'

'I'm sorry, dear,' says the nurse, and then talking to Anna as though she were a child, she tells her, 'Say goodbye to your friend.'

'Goodbye,' Anna says, rather sullenly.

'Goodbye,' Margot replies, a little puzzled and saddened by the incident.

10

Museum Visit

D ANA, who prides herself on her aesthetic sensitivity, always considers that she has a limited time-span of enthusiasm for museum visits and on this occasion, after two hours of looking round Bridchester Museum, her energy is beginning to flag. Mike's, however, is continually renewed by the multitude of objects behind the glass cases.

'I must sit down for a minute,' she sighs. 'My feet are killing me.'

'You're such a philistine,' Mike laughs, escorting her to a bench padded with orange-coloured imitation leather. 'You can quite happily spend hours on end making paper flowers, but when you're faced with genuine antiquities, you'd rather sit on a bench and doze.'

But Dana is already moving towards the garden outside.

'Now that's unfair,' Dana bursts out. 'No, it's worse than that, it's cruel. It's because everything means so much to me that I can't absorb it all in one go. I mean, each object makes me think of so many things. It's just mentally exhausting.'

Mike sits down beside her and stretches out his legs in front of him so they are parallel with the floor.

'Don't do that – you'll trip someone up,' Dana says irritably.

'Not only are you an intellectual moron, but you're a

nagging housewife.'

'I hate the way you come out with those slick phrases,' Dana snaps, 'as though you're mentally making a note of them for some article you're writing.'

'Which I am,' Mike admits with a laugh. 'Very perceptive of you, I must say.'

'Oh, I must look at that case over there,' Dana says, getting up. 'I can see little golden things gleaming at me across the room.'

'That sounds rather twee,' Mike says, accompanying her. 'You're very fickle. One moment you want to sit down and the next you get restless.'

'Yes, sure,' Dana replies with a smile. 'I was the typical fidgety child, if you must know, and I haven't changed. Oh, look at that spoon!' She pointed to a tiny, intricately filigreed gold spoon, shaped like a mandolin. 'That's perfect, just perfect, and some of these reliquaries are just out of this world.'

Tony winces at her superlatives. They jar in his ear. It is unfortunate that Dana and Mike are both word-conscious but in different ways, and this difference only serves to irritate them both. They pass on to a case full of ancient pieces of glassware.

'I love that misty effect,' Dana says. 'You know, if someone were to produce some pieces of modern art glassware like that, they'd sell like a bomb. It often amazes me that artists and designers and art students and people generally don't make more use of ancient designs and techniques. I mean, this vase looks as though it's got a layer of paint on it. The effect is quite fantastic. And this ewer is really unusual.'

Her attention is now drawn to an enormous cross made of sold rock crystal, ornamented around the edges with silver and gold emblems.

'I wonder why it is that all the best pieces of art – no, that's a generalisation, some of the best masterpieces – have been inspired by religious themes.'

'I should think the answer's fairly obvious.'

'No, it isn't. You say that because you just accept things.'

'Look, let's drop the subject,' Tony says placatingly. 'It won't get us anywhere.'

'You're just a conformist. It's so easy to conform.'

'Your readiness to pull down edifices is just as automatic and unthinking as my so-called acceptance of them,' he retorts.

'How dare you speak to me like that!' Dana whispers hoarsely, attempting to control her rage but merely emphasising it because of the redness in her face that whispering in anger produces.

'Oh look!' Mike is not deliberately trying to change the subject but is genuinely diverted. 'Isn't that the woman we saw at that ghastly reception?'

Dana turns round abruptly to see a tall woman in a grey coat approaching them.

'Oh yes!' she says. 'Hi, remember me. I saw you last week at that awful thing at the town hall.'

Alison blinks in surprise and then, recognising her, smiles pleasantly. 'Oh, hello, yes, it was rather awful, wasn't it. I'm afraid you were unlucky in your encounter with Miss Bushnell. She's not always as bad as that, but when she's in a bad temper, she can be pretty offensive.'

'Well, I was rather dumbfounded,' Dana admits.

'It would take a good deal to dumfound you, Dana,'

'Yeah, that's true,' she smiles.

11

William

'WHAT a blood nerve,' exclaims Alison as the door slams behind William.

'I don't think it was a very good idea to put him in here with us,' Paula says. 'I mean, he's not professional and he's only temporary.'`

'Well, June's all right.'

'Oh yes, she's very nice. And I suppose we can't really have the one without the other.'

Two new temporary posts have just been created in the Records Office for two clerks, who are employed to do a little filing, typing and envelope-filling. Margaret Bushnell has been amazed at the response to her new venture and the secretary and treasurer have, in fact, been too inundated with duties to perform all the clerical work themselves.

Miss Bushnell, preoccupied as always with administrative shortcuts, has hit upon the idea of the temporary clerks as an expedient and has had no trouble in filling the vacancies. The two lucky candidates are June Brentwood, awaiting a place at secretarial college, and William Pearce, a dropout sociology student. It is William's views on everything from sex, drugs and rock 'n' roll to politics, religion and virtually everything that have provoked Alison's indignation, not so much by their content as by the bolshy way he expresses them.

Alison eats her sandwiches, glancing occasionally at the clock as the midday sun streams onto her desk.

'Gosh, I could just fall asleep.'

'Why don't you go home and have a nap, you lucky part-timer,' Paula laughs.

'What a glorious thought, but I've got to finish an essay on the effects of enclosures in the fourteenth century. I just don't feel in the mood.'

'Well, there's no shortcut to academic success,' Paula declares with mock pomposity.

'It's not academic success I want. I'll be pleased if just scrape through this bloody degree. Oh, why am I so lazy?'

'No, in fact you're very energetic.'

'I know I give the impression of being energetic, but I'm just disorganised. I like to do what I like and when I feel like it. But at least I'm not proud of my indolence like William is. Did you hear him talking to his friend on the phone?'

'Well, he always seems to be on the phone, as far as I can make out.'

'No, the one about how he spends every Sunday. He was saying he never gets up till four in the afternoon. He thinks the rest is good for him.'

'Perhaps he meditates.'

'No. He was saying he just listens to music all day. He gets my back up so much.'

'That's probably what he's aiming to do.'

'You're probably right, but it doesn't make any difference. It's not really his modus vivendi I object to – it's his complacency. He's as smug as any of the middle-class establishment he claims to object to so violently.'

'Well, you should have heard what he had to say about man's psychological needs,' Paula laughs. 'That was hilarious. Of course, I only got his side of the conversation and what he was saying was tenable, I suppose, but it was the dogmatic way he came out with it. He was talking to this guy about censorship and how evil it is, and was saying that all religion is the result of sexual repression. You'd think he was some kind of oracle. I don't think the chap at the other end had a chance to get a word in sideways.'

The door-handle turns, and both women look up, embarrassed in case it was William, but it's June who enters.

'Had a nice walk?' Alison asks politely.

'Mmm, super,' June replies cheerily. 'It's a gorgeous day outside. What's happened to our little ray of sunshine?' She glances at William's desk.

'Oh, we're just in the middle of one of our usual bitching sessions about him,' Paula says, smiling.

'Well, really. He's enough to drive anyone round the bend,' June says.

'It really infuriates me the way he talks *at* you and not *to* you. He's so conceited.'

'I know,' Alison says. 'Do you know—'

As the door handle turns again, all three look up guiltily, but this time it's Dana.

'Oh er … excuse me,' she says, walking in hesitantly and leaving the door ajar behind her. 'I was wondering—'

'Hello,' Alison says. 'I always seem to be bumping into you.'

'Hi – again! I was just passing and then I remembered that someone said something about there being a clerical job here for the local history society.'

'Oh, what a pity you didn't come last week,' Paula says. 'We had two vacancies, but they've both been taken.'

'Oh, I see... Oh well, it doesn't matter. As I said, I was just passing and the idea occurred to me, but it really doesn't matter.'

'Don't go,' Alison says cordially. 'Stay and have some coffee with us.'

'But I don't want to interrupt you when you're working.'

They all laugh. 'That's a good joke,' Alison says. 'Firstly, it's our lunch break, and secondly, we make it a policy not to work very hard in this establishment.'

'Well, we do work sometimes,' Paula elaborates, 'but we also indulge in long gossip sessions.'

'Sounds like fun,' Dana says.

As Alison goes off to make the coffee, Dana drops a large carrier bag onto the floor and a heap of paper flowers fall out.

'I say,' Paula says. 'What gorgeous flowers. Where did you get them from?'

'Oh, I make them. I have to do something to justify my lazy existence.'

There is the sound of noisy footsteps up the corridor and then William walks in, slamming the door after him.

'They're having a terrific demonstration down Church Parade,' he says, seating himself energetically at his desk.

'I know,' Dana says, 'I was nearly knocked over by it.'

'I'm surprised we can't hear it from here. It's such a racket. The pigs have been busting people left, right and centre. It pisses me off the way the establishment can just do what they want. They're such fascists. I think the police force in this country is a serious threat to our democracy. They're dangerous.'

'Dangerous in what way?' asks Paula.

'Well, it's putting power in the hands of a large organised body of people – power which can easily be corrupted. It's totally undemocratic to give any group of people such power.'

He gets up angrily and slams the window shut. 'This whole place needs reorganising. I've always thought walking out of my course was the most intelligent step I ever took in my life.'

He fiddles around noisily in his desk drawer – 'Oh hell, I've run out of cigarettes' – and runs noisily out of the room.

After William has gone, they all look at each other.

'He's just a little boy pretending to be grown up,' sighs June. 'It's rather pathetic really.'

'Well, I think he's entitled to state his views,' says Dana, whose own views are in many respects similar to William's.

'It's not what he says, but the way he expresses it,' Paula says. 'And it's maddening having a discussion with him, because he just talks over you, so we've all just given up and we have to listen to a barrage of undiluted William all day long.'

'Oh, I see what you mean,' Dana says as Alison re-emerges with the coffee and June hands it round.

'By the way,' Paula says, 'do tell us your name so that if a vacancy does occur, we can let you know.'

'Sure, I'll write it down with my address.' Dana scribbles it down on a scrap of paper and hands it to Paula.

'Oh, are you related to Professor Newsom?'

'Yes,' Dana sighs, 'worse luck. I sometimes feel I have no identity except as the great man's daughter.'

'Oh sorry,' Paula says.

'It's OK,' Dana laughs. 'I'm quite proud of him sometimes, when he gets his head out of all those dusty old tomes and actually says something original, which doesn't happen very often admittedly, but it does occasionally.'

They all laugh and continue to drink their coffees as the church bell opposite strikes two o'clock.

12

At Home
with Dana and Mike

D ANA SITS curled up on the settee, a book propped up above her folded arms, one leg tapping impatiently against the red cloth of the upholstery. Mike sits opposite her in an armchair, stolidly flicking over the pages of the *Times Literary Supplement*. All that can be heard is the soft scuffing sound of Dana's tapping foot, the quiet flicking of pages and the ticking of the clock.

'God, we must do something about that wretched clock,' Dana sighs. 'The way it ticks in that muffled way. It's partly because you can only half hear it that it's so irritating. If it was a normal loud tick I wouldn't mind, but those undertones get on my nerves.'

Mike does not answer, but continues to read, abstractedly twisting the hair at the back of his head into corkscrew curls.

'Oh when are they going to come? It's damned rude to arrive this late and not even to ring with some explanation.'

'That's an illogical statement,' Mike says. 'They haven't yet arrived.'

'Yeah, but you know what I mean. I feel that they're going to arrive and my lovely meal all dried up and horrible. People are so thoughtless and stupid.'

She twists over onto her back and stretches out full length

on the settee, positioning her feet against the arms at the back.

'I'm just in a bad temper as usual,' she sighs.

Mike's failure to reply strikes her as silent assent. 'It's all your fault for inviting them,' she lashes out. 'Who the hell are they anyway? I mean, they're not really friends, are they. You've just invited them because you want to get in with the right people and—'

'Does it matter if they're friends,' Mike says. 'They're just people and I thought people were your passion in life.'

'Yes, well that was true until I discovered how stupid and bloody-minded most people are. Particularly dentists,' she adds sourly.

Mike can't help laughing.

'How can you laugh? How can you be so insensitive?' She throws her book on the floor. She has a dentist appointment next week for three fillings and possibly two extractions.

'When that phone rang from the hospital and I heard you answer it,' she continues, 'my heart sank right to my feet. You know, I could feel it resting between my toes somewhere.'

'Your toes are very sweet.' Mike takes a pen out of his shirt pocket and scribbles a note in the margin of his magazine.

'Gee thanks. And when he told me that three of them were totally bad, I just felt kind of... I don't know I—'

The phone rings and Dana jumps nervously as Mike extends an arm to the table behind and lifts the receiver.

'That'll be them, the fools,' Dana mutters.

'Oh, hello Ma.'

Dana jumps again and runs round to Mike's left elbow, to listen in on the conversation like a small animal, flicking her head this way and that as Mike teasingly moves the phone into odd angles as he talks.

'Fine... I'll see you Sunday then. Goodbye.' He puts the phone down.

'Mike, you're a beast. It's nice to hear from your mother though.'

'Yes,' he replies absently, picking up his magazine again.

Dana continues fidgeting, straightening cushions and placing books and magazines in a neat pile on a lower shelf of the bookcase.

'Yeah, your family are so incredibly nice.'

'Sometimes I think you like my family more than you like me.'

Dana blinks. 'No, not exactly.' She never jokes about personal relationships, particularly when a near truth has been uttered. 'I suppose I've built up a halo-image of them all together in that house, and because I don't know them that well, the illusion hasn't had time to crumble.'

'Sounds very cynical.'

'No, I didn't mean that, but what I mean is, we kind of know each other so well, we can't really have any illusions about each other and so now it's difficult for me to know whether I know you at all, because in a way one's view of another person is totally composed of illusions.'

'So you think if you knew my family better you wouldn't like them so much,' Mike says, yawning behind his right hand.

'Well, it's difficult to say. Now your mother, I'm sure I could possibly be disillusioned about her. She's such a fantastic person – she's not even fantastic, she's just a person, a human being – and my God, it's so difficult just to be that nowadays. Most people are aping other people, but just to exist and to be is very difficult in itself.'

'Yes, Ma's got a streak of individuality that would appeal to you. She was quite a rebel in her youth.'

'Oh, Mike, you've totally misunderstood what I was saying,' Dana says irritably.

'No, I haven't. I just added that as an afterthought.'

'Sometimes I think I pick on what you say like a broody hen scratching around amongst the corn,' she laughs. 'You know, I can just imagine myself as an old lady, very clean and neat and washed, but very grumpy. "Come along in, dear, but don't make too much noise."'

'You didn't get the toothless effect. Make it a bit more sybilant.'

'Oh, Mike, you're cruel. Why did you have to remind me? Oh God, teeth!' She flops back onto the settee. 'Teeth and bloody people – they make me sick!'

Mike laughs and scribbles another note in the margin.

13

Class, Code and Control

PAULA folds up a copy of the minutes of the last meeting.

'I think I'm gong to resign from this wretched committee,' she declares. 'All these amendments to amendments of the third proposal are getting me down. What is it about committee work, I wonder, that makes people get like that?'

'It's an affliction that seems to descend on the middle-aged,' Dana comments wryly. 'I've seen it happen on many occasions.'

Since her last visit, she has taken to popping in to the Records Office unannounced for coffee and a chat with the staff, who welcome the diversion.

'Well, I'm still in my prime,' Paula says petulantly, 'and I'm not going to let it happen to me. Honestly, it takes up hours of my time and it's such a bore.'

'You obviously haven't got the right attitude,' Alison says, breaking off from her typing for a minute. 'I mean, don't you realise you're furthering a highly academic enterprise?'

'Academic hoo-ha,' Paula snorts.

'Balderdash and codswollop, guys.'

'William, must you talk like something out of Williamy Bunter?' June laughs.

'Slang is often more expressive than formal vocabulary. I refer you to Basil Bernstein, *Class, Code and Control* on the semantic significance of classroom language.'

'You're not a sociology student now,' June retorts.

'Fortunately for me. Most universities are fascist organisations like the fuzz—'

'It's just not fair,' Paula says, returning to their previous conversation. 'Why should I have to spend all my time slogging away for a menial wage—'

'You think you've got problems.' Alison resumes her typing, having the ability to type and talk at the same time, even if both processes are slowed down as a result. 'I nearly walked out on Steve last night. In the end I stayed, but I've threatened to find a flat on my own somewhere.'

She looks round and sees them staring open-mouthed at her in a mixture of surprise and polite sympathy.

'Well, it's hopeless. We're completely incompatible. I've known it all along, but now I'm just sick of pretending. Our relationship is a fiasco, the whole thing.'

'It's easier to find a flat on one's own than it is if you're sharing,' Paula suggests. She herself has been lucky to find a compatible flatmate in Deirdre, especially as Deirdre is often out. They get along very well, but she likes to have her own space, and time to herself, away from other people – including Douglas.

William, however, is evidently considering the sociological implications of Alison's statement. 'I don't think it's you or him, and I don't think you're incompatible. That's not the trouble. The real problem is that marriage is a dying institution. It's no longer valid in this day and age. You can't expect two people to live together for years on end. It's totally un-natural.

Alison darts him a look of pure contempt. 'William, with the best will on the world, what do you know about whether we're compatible or not? Fuck all, I would venture to say. And in any case, we're not married, as it so happens. We've hardly been living together for a lifetime – it's only been two and a half years.'

She sighs and drops her typing, which has gradually slowed down to the occasional hypnotic beat, and cups her head in her hands. Her hair is spread over her shoulders, ruf-fled as usual, with silky strands emerging from a cloud of fluffy tangles.

'Oh well,' she says, 'that's life, I suppose.'

June laughs. 'You remind me of my granddad. He always used to sigh and declare "'That's life,"' whenever anyone said anything controversial. It was his way of dealing with a situa-tion that actually required you to think. It always used to make me giggle.'

'A lot of people deal with intellectual dilemmas like that, William says. 'They just shelve the problem or give in or keep well out of it. They're too frightened to participate and take a stand. That's the trouble with the majority of the population today. They're too worried about their security and reputa-tion to really give an honest opinion. I mean, there's no real communication.'

Paula, who is gradually coming round to liking William, even if his dogmatism irritates her, nods in agreement. 'It's like when you get on a train. You see everybody wearing completely closed expressions and it's only when something unusual happens like a hold-up or the lights going out, that they actually come to life and talk.'

'It's the English educational system that's at fault,' William says, assuming a tone of sagelike infallibility. 'We're too inhibited. We've got past the stage of caring about things like long hair on men, but we're still completely hidebound in other respects.'

'Yes,' Paula nods. 'It's sad really. It's awful when you think of the people who live next door to each other and never communicate except for the occasional hello.'

'Oh God,' Alison exclaims. 'Who wants to communicate with their neighbours? I mean, some people are such bloody bores. One may not be able to choose one's family, but at least one can choose one's friends.'

'It's not a question of friendship,' William says. 'It goes beyond personal relationships. It's a question of general communication between people en masse. It simply doesn't happen, except in the case of crowd hysteria and in that situation it's usually fanatical or violent or whatever. No, what I'd like to see is people expressing themselves fully and really getting down to a proper—'

'Oh no,' Alison interrupts, 'silence is better sometimes. I don't see any virtue in communication for its own sake. Most of it is twaddle—'

'It isn't,' William disagrees, his voice rising angrily, 'it's only twaddle because people don't talk properly. They abuse the powers of speech. If they really talked it would be fantastic.'

'But you can't change people,' Alison insists, flushing with indignation. 'You can't order people to have high-powered intellectual conversations to order, instead of gossip. They'll simply talk in the manner they've been accustomed to and—'

'I'm not saying they should have *intellectual* conversations.' William emphasises the word 'intellectual' dismissively. 'You're distorting my words.'

'There's a lack of communication going on somewhere,' June remarks facetiously.

'No, what I was saying,' William persists like a dog with a bone, 'is that people should really open themselves up.'

Alison groans and they all laugh.

'Well, I'd rather close myself up,' Alison says. 'Speaking of interpersonal relationships, sometimes I think that psychology and sociology have become almost pseudo-religions, the way people follow them so avidly.'

'Don't put it down to psychology and sociology,' William raises his voice as though taking this as a personal insult. 'That's just labelling things.'

'Ssshhh, William,' Paula says. 'Miss Bushnell will hear you if you make too much noise.'

'Yes, all those ancient academics in the searchroom will be disturbed in their scholastic studies,' Alison says.

'What I meant was—' William starts to say.

'Oh shut up,' Alison breaks in, 'I don't want to communicate and you'll jolly well have to accept it.'

Paula blushes at Alison's bluntness and they all return to their respective occupations in an uneasy silence.

14

A Bit of a Debate

D ANA walks gingerly into the town hall annexe for the debate on 'This House Believes that Press Sensationalism Does Harm to the Traditions of Bridchester Journalism and to Our Local Culture', conducted jointly by the Bridchester Press Guild and the Bridchester Local History Society.

Michael Brennan has insisted on speaking against the motion, seconded by the Press Guild chairman; speaking for the motion are Professor Humphrey Newsom and Margot's husband, Tony Harrison.

Dana spots Margot, whom she met at a previous meeting, halfway down the room, with Anna sitting listlessly by her side. Dana taps Margot on the shoulder and sits down on her other side.

'Hi,' she says.

'Hello,' Margot replies in her soft Virginian accent, which for some reason sounds less pronounced than Dana's Canadian accent.

'God, I hate these affairs,' Dana says. 'I always get so nervous when Mike's involved in anything. He never seems to care. It's ridiculous really. Here am I sitting shaking all over with clammy hands, and he's been as calm as a summer sea all day long.'

'That's an interesting analogy,' Anna suddenly says.

Dana is surprised as Anna had not looked as though she had been listening. Margot, meanwhile, feels slightly embarrassed at Anna's social gaucheness and immediately feels ashamed at her own reaction.

'Sure, I know what you mean,' she says, replying to Dana. 'Tony gets a bit nervy beforehand, but I always think he does better when he's wound up. Tell me, are you still feeling browned off with doing nothing?'

Dana blinks with mild surprise. It is unlike Margot to make such direct personal remarks like this.

'Well, I'm not quite doing nothing ... but yes,' she admits reluctantly, 'I'm kind of tearing my hair out all day and getting told off by Mike and by my father and it seems just about everybody on all sides, so of course I react by quarrelling like mad with them all and being totally impossible.'

She laughs gleefully as she reflects on her general disagreeability over the past four weeks.

'Well, I'll tell you why I'm asking,' Margot explains. 'I want to write a biography of the Fourth Earl of Bridchester, who lived here in the manor in the mid-sixteenth century, and I need a bit of a help in doing research and assembling material. It's quite a big undertaking and I don't know how much longer we'll be living in this part of the world. Tony's the sort of guy who's perfectly capable of uprooting himself all of a sudden and once he's finished this wretched thesis, I suppose he might get offered a job somewhere else.'

'Yes, I see,' Dana says sympathetically.

'I suppose in a way, it's a bit ambitious to undertake such a vast project under the circumstances, but I've always enjoyed writing and recently I have felt a sort of creative urge, so I have been doing character sketches and short stories and poems and so on, but I feel my real medium should be biography—'

'Yes, everybody has their own particular literary medium,' Anna breaks in.

'That's quite true,' Dana says. 'I suppose mine is reduced to making paper flowers and batique scarves at the moment.'

Margot laughs but Anna doesn't respond, as though she either hasn't heard or an invisible wall lies between her and the other two women, preventing her from communicating with them.

'So I suppose really it's about time I broadened my horizons, as they say,' Dana continues. 'Yes, you know I think I *would* like to help you. I'd enjoy doing the research. I adore scrabbling around with ancient manuscripts and things. For one thing I've got very good sight and I know that may sound funny, but in fact it's very useful, as far as dealing with archives and records is concerned.'

'Oh yes, I agree. Well, I am very pleased that you're so enthusiastic. I wasn't sure what your reaction would be.'

'Yeah. Well, you just happened to catch me at the right time. I must tell you that I'm one of these people, who attract pieces of good luck at the right time.' Dana laughs. 'It always seems to happen to me when my batteries are kind of running down and all my inner resources are used up and then something happens to create a new channel of self-expression.'

Margot laughs. 'That sounds kind of quaint, but I know what you mean.'

'I'm quite the opposite,' Anna says. 'I find that interesting things always seem to happen to me at once, and then I'm left with big gaps and nothing to do.'

Margot smiles sympathetically – Anna seems quite alert tonight, though as usual her ability to be a part of a conversation is sporadic and unpredictable.

'Well, look, Anna,' Dana says warily. 'Would you like to help too?'

Margot looks worried.

'It would be nice if Anna did a little bit of the writing for us,' Dana suggests.

'Yes, I'd like to,' Anna replies with a hopeful smile.

'It sounds a good idea,' Margot agrees, 'though maybe it would be best if we didn't give you too much to do.'

'But a little of it would be fun,' Anna says. 'I don't believe in getting back to my studies at the moment, but I feel I could get interested in an individual project, particularly something imaginative like this one.'

'Jolly good.' Dana suddenly sounds very English.

At this point, they have to stop talking as the debate is about to begin. Looking up and seeing Mike and her father seated on either side of the chairman, Dana thinks that her loyalties really ought to be divided – and yet, as she has to admit to herself, her feelings for both speakers are negligible. She ascribes this to a natural coldness combined with her recent irritability, which has soured her feelings towards people generally.

Dana thinks hurriedly how best to describe to herself her present mood: 'acid' seems to be an appropriate word, though perhaps not precise enough. During the debate, her mind flits from topic to topic, sometimes lingering on the debate in progress, sometimes on her own predicament..

'The purpose of the press is to provide us with information,' she hears her father say. 'Straightforward information so that we can then form our own opinions on it. We do not want this information so distorted before it reaches us, so that there is no possibility of each of us interpreting it according to his or her individual viewpoint, which should be the aim of visual communication.

'The techniques that are employed by the press to step up circulation result in a vicious circle, in that the public who are fed a daily diet of exaggerated features about sex, crime and the personal lives of celebrities, come to want more and more of it. Not only does the press not provide the information required of it, but it does so in such a way as to lower the reading tastes of the public, which indeed has the effect of contaminating their minds.'

Dana yawns: this is all typical of her father – obvious opinions tritely expressed, though with a modicum of sincerity. It does not display the scholastic originality and ingenuity that had won him his chair. She always feels sorry for him when he attempts to speak about non-academic questions, for although he never puts forward a foolish argument, he certainly never displays any of his creative fire.

She begins to ponder on the effects of that creative fire on the individual. She wonders how far Margot's project will succeed. It certainly seems an interesting position and might be a good hobby for Anna. The real problem is whether they will manage to complete the undertaking, or whether they will get bogged down by it.

But the idea presents many possibilities: both the idea of historical research and the possibility of reconstructing a historical personality appeals to Dana greatly. She would like to become personally involved in a world removed from the twentieth century, for the latter certainly does not appeal to her. *I'm just a critical old misfit*, she thinks to herself and then smiles wryly because, in fact, she knows that she is proud of being so.

15

The Third Earl

PAULA rushes up the stairs, through the corridor and into the office to find that everybody has settled down to work. It is an uncomfortable feeling to be late, particularly on a Monday morning, when one has to grow accustomed to the rhythm of work again after the leisurely inactivity of the weekend. Her forehead is furrowed with annoyance and her dark, thin face looks sallow and tired.

'Had a nice weekend?' Alison says, looking up from her typing.

'Lousy,' Paula replies, and goes into the adjoining office to collect some material. She returns to find Alison sitting bolt upright, her chin propped between her hands, obviously waiting for an outpouring of Paula's troubles.

Paula laughs. 'You do look funny.'

'Thank you. I wish I could do something about it.'

'No, you know what I mean.' Paula briskly turns over the pages of a parish register. 'You look as though you want me to have a sob-session all over the office.'

The others laugh. 'Do tell us,' June says. 'We're all dying to hear.'

Paula smiles ruefully. 'Oh well, everything went wrong.' She sorts through the drawer flinging paper into the waste bin. 'I mean, those college reunions are always ghastly. I suppose Dana thought I'd actually enjoy going to the May Ball, but I didn't. When we got to Cambridge, we met dozens of her cronies, and they all got on my nerves.

'I suppose Saturday wasn't all that bad. They had a huge marquee and strawberries and cream, and sherry – actually I drank rather too much sherry. I certainly felt very malevolently disposed towards mankind in general and Douglas in particular. I don't know, he was really irritating me. Then on Sunday we went to Ely to have lunch with his parents and oh...' She pulls a face.

'What happened?'

'Well, nothing. That's the trouble. I can't put my finger on anything, but basically I realised that we just aren't compatible. When we're by ourselves we have a fairly amicable working relationship – I think he tones down his personality for my benefit – but when he's with his parents, he's dreadful. And they're so possessive. They expect him to conform to all their ideas and opinions. And he more or less does.

'Anyway, I got involved in a very long-winded and pointless argument with them about women's rights – essentially they didn't think women should have any rights at all except the right to be in the kitchen and cook dinners for their husbands. And Douglas took their side. I got so furious with them that I really lost my temper. Needless to say, they were distinctly off me after that, and Douglas was chilly to say the least...'

'Jesus, I can just imagine it all,' Alison says sympathetically. 'You poor thing. You must have had a terrible time.'

'Well, towards the end I began to quite enjoy it. We were all going round the place frightfully restrained and chilly and bottled up, so by yesterday evening I was getting rather giggly – it was just a hysterical reaction, but they clearly didn't approve of that either. It's left me feeling like a wet rag—'

'Which is the perfect way to start a Monday morning,' Alison laughs. 'Fortunately we don't seem to be too inundated with work today.'

'Oh well, that's some small blessing, I suppose. Anyway, I've got to see Maggie about a new donation that's due to arrive tomorrow. It's a collection of documents belonging to the Duke of Bridchester – the Third Earl – in the mid-sixteenth century. It's actually very interesting.'

'Isn't that the one who was killed after falling off his horse?' William says.

'Yes, that's him. He was thrown off very violently and at a relatively early age – I think he was forty-seven. But in fact he was a very unusual character. He wrote poetry, including hymns and carols. He was also a philanthropist and did a lot of benevolent work for the poor in the district.'

'Well, they certainly needed it,' Alison says. 'Honestly, when you look at those poor rate returns and pauper removal orders, you realise the extent of the problem. We're very lucky to have cured it to the extent that we have.'

'You must be kidding,' William says. 'There's a vast hidden underclass of poor people – they just go under the radar and aren't even reported in government statistics.'

'In that case, how do you know they exist?' June asks.

'For that I would refer you to Townsend and Abel-Smith in *The Poor and the Poorest*. And when you think of the current unemployment problems in Ireland—'

'OK, OK, you're probably right,' Alison says impatiently, 'but you've got to admit it's not nearly such a wide-scale problem as it was.'

'Define your terms. What do you mean by wide-scale—'

'I haven't told you the most interesting thing about our sixteenth-century duke,' Paula says.

Even William is stopped in his tracks. They stare at Paula expectantly.

'It seems Robert, Duke of Bridchester, had a most extraordinary and quite unusual love affair – and incidentally, one that was completely unrequited. And surprisingly the object of his affections wasn't some young, rich, beautiful aristocratic woman—'

'Oh, was he queer?' William says.

'No, nothing like that. He fell for a young woman while he was administering to the poor in the shire. She may have been illiterate or semi-literate, but it seems he taught her to read and she then became the subject – or the object – of some quite scorchingly passionate love letters.

'Her name was Grace and it looks as though he first met her only a couple of years before his death. So the "unrequited" aspect was possibly not just about their difference in age and class and financial status, but that he was actually quite a romantic, not to say gallant and gentlemanly soul, and wished to woe her in accordance with courtly tradition. And it looks as though, against all the advice and wishes of his family, he was about to propose to her when fate intervened – and he was thrown off that horse, which of course put an end to all his hopes and dreams – and presumably hers.'

There is silence for a few seconds. Even William seems lost for words.

'How sad,' June says. 'How beautiful.'

'I wish I'd known him,' Alison says.

William has pulled himself together, 'Essentially though he was a parasite, freeloading off the state and—'

'Shut up!' the women shout in unison.

16

Memories of Poole Street

MARGOT watches Tony screwing up pieces of paper and throwing the whole lot into the waste bin. He smiles sheepishly as he retrieves a large brown envelope.

'Your letters to me when you were living in Poole Street,' he says. Putting them back in the bureau, he tidies the remaining heap of papers and goes into the next room to continue his studies. Margot is grateful that he has placed a sentimental value upon her letters, particularly because he is normally scornful of sentimentality and any form of distorted or exaggerated emotion.

But although it pleases her, she is instantly saddened and depressed by the thought of the contrast between their former deep intimacy – those long conversations when they lived in Poole Street – and their present relatively distant relationship, always the same brief verbal exchanges due to lack of time and the morass of daily routine to be managed

Poole Street was a small street in London's Kentish Town, where Margot rented a large bedsit on the second floor while working on her doctorate. She had put an ad in a literary journal asking for information about an eighteenth-century Member of Parliament, a Whig and something of a rake, upon whom her thesis was centred.

Tony had replied, offering to lend her a book on the subject, which might prove valuable. They had met to discuss the matter in a local café and after a few polite remarks, Margot had discovered that Tony needed a particular book on the history of racial conflict and segregation in the States, which she happened to have, so an exchange of books was agreed.

The snow was falling thickly on the pavements as they approached her flat and Margot's skin, normally pale and lifeless, glowed pink and shiny under the frozen crystals cascading from the windblown branches. Tony was about to dine with work colleagues that evening, and as they climbed the stairs, Margot had giggled stupidly at her own casual appearance in jeans and sheepskin jacket and his formal black suit.

When she reached her room her numb fingers were beginning to thaw and she rubbed them against her hips. Tony had shifted in embarrassment from one foot to the other as he waited to collect the book, while Margot was trying to restore normality to her white fingers, and he had eventually sat down gingerly at the end of her settee while she made coffee. Through the windows, the black branches gradually disappeared as they were whitewashed by snow and the white sky glared in bleak, brilliant contrast to the orange glow of the electric fire and red carpet.

Tony had been attracted to Margot's vitality and liveliness, and as she busied herself tidying the room, making it comfortable for him, he had at last relaxed and started to talk at great length about his work as a journalist and researcher. Margot had been a sympathetic and responsive listener.

She often regrets that Tony doesn't talk to her as frequently now as he had then, for she has a receptive mind that needs the stimulus of others and their ideas for her to come to life and she finds it difficult to be creative in a vacuum. Hence, her interest in writing the biography of the Duke of Bridchester not only stems from her fascination with the man himself but also the opportunity to work with others, who, it now seems, will be Dana and Anna.

Margot remembers Tony's enthusiasm, his expansiveness, as he sat in his admittedly dusty black suit, flushed and smiling. That window of communication between them currently seems to be more or less closed, but she is determined to reopen it, and is hoping that her new research project will at least stimulate her own mind and possibly Tony will be stimulated into the bargain.

As she stands by the oak table in the living room speculating, Tony re-enters and, as if divining her thoughts, looks down at her and says, 'Is something the matter?'

'Oh, er … well, no, I was just kind of thinking…'

She is unwilling for some reason to communicate with him at this moment, or perhaps is simply unable to do so. She sighs and makes an effort.

'It's just that we've kind of changed a lot recently.'

Tony remains standing, staring at her. 'I know,' he says. 'Does it matter? People change and develop. You can't remain standing in one spot, you know.'

'Oh sure, but I feel we've lost something,' she says tentatively.

'No, nothing's been lost. I mean, obviously I don't go round saying "I love you" the whole time, but that's because I presume you know it. Verbage is garbage, remember,' he adds, alluding to a feeble joke made on occasions by Margot's father.

Margot laughs half-heartedly. 'It isn't garbage for a start. It's simply that we're always in such a rush these—'

'Who isn't,' he breaks in and then, seeing the unhappy look on her face, puts his arms around her and gives her a long, passionate kiss.

'Oh Tony,' Margot says eventually, 'I feel like a second-rate character out of some old-time Douglas Fairbanks movie, talking about our relationship and moping around all over the place.'

'Don't be so self-conscious about the effect you're making. It's not important.'

She smiles, relieved that at least they have re-established their old familiarity.

'I know. I'm quite surprised that—'

'Mummy!' Hilary wails, rushing into the room and hurling herself at Margot, who pulls away from Tony and picks her up. 'Mummy, I've lost my spoon! My spoon!'

The spoon in question is a large pink plastic one, to which Hilary has become inextricably attached in recent times.

'Oh Hilary, we'll find it. Come along now.'

Margot goes off to Hilary's room, still holding her daughter aloft, while Tony scratches his head thoughtfully as he returns to his study.

17

Skeleton in the Cupboard

THE PHONE rings on the table by Alison's desk. She leaps up to answer it, while the others listen to her conversation, hearing a series of 'yes'es, punctuated by 'ohs'.

'Sounds intriguing,' June says.

'And monosyllabic to say the least,' William adds.

'We are awful,' laughs Paula, 'The poor woman's probably having a terrible time keeping a straight face.'

Alison gesticulates to them to keep quiet. Eventually she puts down the phone and walks lifelessly over to her desk.

'Oh dear,' she says, sitting down slowly and flicking strands of hair off her face and onto her shoulders.

'What's happened?' asks Paula.

'Well, apparently Steve's mother has just sold her house, because she was going to share with two other friends. and now their plans have fallen through so she's got nowhere to stay.'

'Does that mean that you've got to put her up?'

'I suppose so.'

'For how long?'

'Well, not indefinitely, I hope.'

Alison flicks through her address book and makes a series of shorthand notes in a large, rather tatty pad. Paula knows her well enough to recognise the signs: Alison can blow hot and cold, becoming totally hysterical over trivial incidents and then remaining cool in a crisis, and as she works at her desk through the afternoon she seems to exude an aura of relaxed cheerfulness. Paula makes a mental note that Alison has seemed much more calm and placid recently. That presumably indicates that her studies are going well.

They work in steady silence. Listening to the hush, June is conscious of the occasional twittering of birds and the slow rumble of a distant lorry. Alison hears only the erratic shuffling of the pages of her book as she turns them over.

Each of them emits occasional noises as they work. Alison sometimes tut-tuts, while William taps his pen against the desk. But all these minor sounds seem to be engulfed in a blanket of quiet that hangs over them all protectively, as if cocooning them from the disturbances of the outside world. So it is not surprising that they all jump and look up slightly bewildered as the door bursts open and Dana rushes in.

'Hi, hope you don't mind me popping in again and disturbing you all when you're working.'

'No, of course not,' Alison replies. 'We're used to being interrupted and it's lovely to see you.'

'Gee thanks,' Dana laughs. 'You probably know I'm researching into the life of Robert, Duke of Bridchester. It's absolutely—'

'And the lovely Grace?' William says.

'Yes, how did you know?'

'I've been telling them the little I know about Robert,' Paula explains. 'We recently had a donation of collection of his personal documents and it seems to be a fascinating story. I'll let you know when they're ready for use.'

'Thanks – actually there's quite a bit of stuff on him already.'

'I was always rather keen on that one,' Paula says. 'He was quite a benevolent gentleman – very romantic and quite dishy in to the bargain. Have you seen the painting of him at Bridchester Hall? And as for his love life…'

'I'm surprised it hasn't been turned into a Hollywood movie,' Dana agrees. 'So romantic – and tragic of course with that fatal fall on the horse. But I'm also absolutely amazed at the enormous number of good works and charitable deeds he performed. God, it's quite horrifying. It makes one feel incredibly worldly and profane to read about someone like that.'

They all laugh.

'He sounds too good to be true,' William yawns. 'I'm sure he had a few skeletons in his cupboard.'

'Well, there is—' Dana began.

'There's no point in feeling guilty, Dana,' Alison says comfortingly. 'We all know what an evil person you are.'

'Oh well, you know what I mean,' Dana grins. She is wearing a brown and pink printed smock which, because of its fullness, hangs loosely on her slim figure. 'I've had this curious feeling recently that one shouldn't assess people, not even remotely, which makes my academic work on the above gentleman somewhat difficult.'

'Why shouldn't we assess people?' asks William.

'Well, I mean it's so impossible and so wrong to make value judgments. It's much better to remain completely neutral if you can.'

'History and literature would be pretty watered down if everybody felt that way,' William replies. 'You're setting an impossibly high standard.'

'I know I am,' Dana retorts and tossing back her head adds with mock solemnity, 'and it's a pity more people don't these days. We're living in an age of decadence – not to say depravity.'

'Speaking of depravity, how are—' William begins.

'Don't speak of depravity,' Dana declares histrionically. 'I don't want to hear about it. I just want to hear about nice, simple things and nice simple people.'

'Like the Duke of Bridchester,' Alison says, 'who's going to emerge whiter than white in your biography, not a blemish or stain on his character from the sounds of it.'

'Oh no, he won't really,' Dana replies. 'I don't act according to my principles, I regret to say. No, I've already thought of some pretty interesting interpretations not just of the motives behind his charitable activities but possibly about the true nature of his relationship with Grace. I think he was suffering from a massive guilt complex and wanted to relieve his conscience, so in fact he aimed at high ideals and acted accordingly, but underneath he was feeling deeply guilty all the time.'

'Why should he have felt guilty?' Paula asks disbelievingly.

'Well, I was going to tell you earlier but you interrupted me. It's actually quite interesting. There's a story. which we're gradually piecing together from all the evidence, that when he was a child – well, about ten, I guess – he accidentally caused his baby brother's death by not keeping an eye on him, when they were left alone together, because the nanny was suddenly taken ill, and this baby got scalded to death and—'

'It all sounds pretty far-fetched,' Alison says.

'What's far-fetched about it?' Paula says. 'People were exactly the same in those days as they are now. We tend to think of them as cardboard figures, but I believe that—'

She is interrupted by Miss Bushnell walking in, looking and sounding even more brisk and alert than usual.

'Oh Paula,' she says. 'We've got a gentleman here from Japan who would like to see the searchroom. I thought you could show him round as I have an urgent appointment with Professor Newsom.'

'Give him my regards,' Dana says.

'Oh... er...' she falters.

'He's my father. Tell him that I've started on a project – a historical project. He ought to approve of that.' She smiles smugly.

Oh, er... yes, of course.' The Head Archivist's face expresses a mixture of surprise, disbelief and disapproval. 'Well, I'm pleased to see that our intake of visitors has stepped up quite considerably over the past few months. I've just been comparing the figures for this year and last year and there's a marked improvement.'

She gives an equally smug smile and walks smartly out of the room.

18

Anna on the Lawns

ANNA has started to grow tired of sticking the chips of stone onto the vase. The occasional chatter of the other patients has also begun to irritate her, not because they chat, but because it is occasional, so that when she starts to think about something, she is jerked out of her thoughts by a platitude such as 'What a lovely jug, Mrs Bennett,' or 'I'd rather be doing something energetic than fiddling around with these little things.'

After trying to concentrate for several minutes she grows restless and walks slowly out of the occupational therapy hut into the grounds of the hospital. She makes her way towards her favourite bench in the middle of the lawns.

She sits down at one end of it, savouring the sense of openness and space this location gives her and tries to recreate in her mind the image of the Duke of Bridchester. She has seen the painting of him in Bridchester Hall – it is a little reminiscent of Nicholas Hilliard's flowery, elegant, springlike 'Young Man Amongst Roses', though having been painted a few decades before, in the early years of the Elizabethan era it is not quite so elaborate and is more in the style of Walter Devereux, the First Earl of Essex.

Her imagination, always too vivid, is able to transport him onto a horse and make him ride directly over the grass in front of her. Is he on his way, perhaps to propose to Grace as he takes that fatal ride?

She starts as she sees the figure of a man approach. It seems for a moment as though her fantasy has materialised before her eyes, but then she realises that the man has simply walked across the lawns and has just happened to reach her point of vision at this particular moment. She vaguely remembers him from somewhere, but is not sure where.

'Hello,' he says, approaching and sitting down heavily on the bench. He appears to be in his late twenties and is short and stocky with a doglike, belligerent expression on his face, which is made comical by a small ginger beard. His breath smells a little of whisky, which suggests he is probably not one of the patients as they are not allowed to drink.

'Have you been visiting someone?' she asks.

'Yes, Colin Phillips.'

'Oh yes, I know him,' Anna says vaguely. 'What do you do?'

He is clearly surprised at the question, as people often are until they get used to her interrogative approach, which is her only successful means of opening conversations with new acquaintances.

'Er, I'm a journalist.'

'Oh, do you know Mike Brennan?'

He looks startled.

'He's the boyfriend of a friend of mine,' she explains.

He gazes at her with a certain amount of suspicion and distrust, and then relenting says with a smile, 'I *am* Mike Brennan. I gather you know Dana.'

'Oh goodness,' Anna is overwhelmed with surprise and confusion. 'Are you really? God, what a fantastic coincidence.'

'How do you come to know Dana?' he persists gently.

'Well, I'm helping her on a historical project.'

'Oh yes. She did mention something about it.'

Dana has in fact told him very little about it and has omitted any mention of Anna, sensing correctly that he would disapprove of her involvement in it.

'Well, it's nice to have met you.' He smiles cordially, extending a hand for her to shake. 'I only hope you don't find the project too exhausting. I'm sure they'll understand if you can only put in a few hours here and there. It's more important for you to get yourself better, you know.'

'I know,' she says. 'Some days I feel completely normal and other days... I sort of relapse. But I'm hoping the study will improve my powers of concentration. You see, quite frankly, I don't feel like resuming my formal studies yet... though I suppose I ought to soon.'

As he looks at her she senses an expression of genuine understanding on his face, as if the barrier between them, which always seems to arise when she is with other people, has broken down.

'That's the spirit,' he says. 'Keep your chin up. Well, I'll probably be seeing you again. Bye.'

'Goodbye.'

She waves at him a few minutes later as he turns the corner into the main road. She thinks that it is a strange coincidence that her thoughts about the Duke of Bridchester have materialised into meeting Mike, who is indirectly connected with her project, and then she wonders obscurely whether the forces of time and space could be penetrated by the power of historical research,

She senses that her imagination is running away with her as usual, and abruptly discontinues this line of thought and makes her way back to the occupational therapy hut. The same group of people are still there, each occupied with their own task, but now their absorption and fitful conversation no longer irritate her and she resumes her work on the vase with a vigour that verges on enthusiasm.

19

How to be Happy
in Three Easy Lessons

'WE'RE GOING to Rome at Christmas!' Alison announces. 'I'm terrifically excited about it. It really will be fabulous, especially as there won't be so many tourists as there are in the summer, I hope. Gosh, I can't wait to explore it all.'

'I have very dismal memories of Rome,' June declares. 'Tom and I went there in the height of summer and stayed in a particularly grotty hotel. The taps didn't work in the bath and the whole place was infested with cockroaches. Apart from that side of it, I didn't enjoy the sightseeing at all because I was so debilitated by the heat. Never again!'

'Oh, I don't mind the heat, Actually I'd rather it was very hot than very cold, but I can't bear crowds.'

'Well, the place won't exactly be empty,' June laughed. 'I remember one day I was thrown out of a church because my skirt was considered too short. You'll have to be careful of that.'

'Yes, I know all about that. I was brought up as a Catholic, though I'm not one now.'

'Probably a reaction.'

'Oh, it's just too easy to say that. That's what's so awful about psychology. One never knows whether anything is genuine or just a reaction or what.'

'I'm sorry. I didn't mean to be personal.'

'Oh, that's all right. I suppose I feel guilty about being an atheist.'

'Really,' says Paula, who has walked into the room in time to catch Alison's last sentence. 'There's no need to feel guilty about things like that.'

'I'd like to go to Mass one of these days,' Alison says. 'I feel I ought to, in a way. Dana was telling me that Margot goes sometimes.'

'Yes, I can imagine that,' Paula says.

'And Anna also goes. That's how Margot met her.'

'What do you think of this project of theirs?'

'Well, it sounds like a good idea. I mean, it might not come off, but it can't do any harm. And I'm sure it's good for Anna to be working with other people. She looks scared stiff most of the time, poor kid.'

'She's not exactly a kid – she's twenty, I think,' June says. 'But I know what you mean: she still looks more like a girl than a woman – even though she can sometimes look almost middle-aged.'

'I suppose that could be the medication,' Paula says.

'Anyway, I should think Dana's dad's pretty pleased about the project,' say June.

'If he knows anything about it, that is,' Alison says. 'I gather she's not on very friendly terms with him. I shouldn't imagine he approves of her way of life.'

'No, it does show a distinct lack of discipline and organisation,' Paula agrees, 'which is what we'd all be drifting into

114

most likely, if we weren't forced to earn our bread and butter,'

'Oh, I wouldn't,' Alison reacts indignantly.

'Well, I'd just love to have the whole day to myself to do what I want and study what I want. I think a combination of external freedom and inner discipline is what I'm most seeking.'

'Sounds good,' June laughs, 'but it's so easy to just drift if you don't have some kind of a purpose in life.'

She thinks about the primary school teaching she has abandoned and wonders for a moment whether a temporary clerical job can possibly be considered as finding her true purpose in life. So is she still just drifting?

'Yes, it sounds like an article from a woman's magazine,' Paula admits. '"How to be Happy in Three Easy Lessons – My Recipe for Success."'

They all laugh.

'God, it's awful to be cooped up in here on a day like this, isn't it,' sighs Alison, who just wants to stretch out in the sun and dream.

'Oh, I rather like it,' William says. 'It's bound to be a hassle out there, sweaty people rushing around in the heat, dogs shitting all over the place, when they're not busy fucking other dogs—'

'Please, William,' June says, 'there are ladies present.'

'What's wrong with plain words? What's in a word anyway? We've become hypersensitive to words. It reflects the unreality of modern social discourse.'

Alison heaves a sigh. She cannot bear William's sociological outbursts, partly because he never allows anyone to argue with him, and because it all sounds so secondhand.

'Back to work, girls and boys,' Paula resumes her often forgotten rank of seniority.

A collective sigh ensues, and silence is restored.

20

Clean Night

PAULA is having a 'clean night'. This ritual involves a bath, washing her hair, and cleaning her kitchen, bathroom and living room. Paula's flat, which is on the ground floor of a large mid-Victorian mansion in north Bridchester, provides her with endless delight, in spite of its ramshackled condition, which offers considerable scope for improvement,

Like Alison, Paula comes from a fairly wealthy family background and attended a girls' boarding school, which was run on the principle that a certain amount of luxury and pampering would not harm the children of the rich, provided it was tempered by equal amounts of discipline and mental and physical exercise.

Hence the dilapidated condition of the flat still seems to her to be a pleasant novelty. She has recently attended a lecture on the 'psychology of geography', in which the theory was put forward that people function best in the type of environment to which they are accustomed, but this does not seem to apply in Paula's case.

She remembers this theory as she deposits several bags of rubbish in the large dustbin in the front garden. She surveys the overgrown, weed-ridden lawn, the sad-looking, uncared for shrubs and bushes, knotted together in painful clumps, and tries to evoke a feeling of Bohemianism about it all, but wryly has to admit to herself that the garden is not quaint and charming, just unkempt and neglected.

When, back in the flat a few minutes later, the phone rings, she jumps expectantly, hoping that it might be Douglas, but it turns out to be a wrong number. Paula and Douglas agreed last week to a trial separation for three weeks and this has, in fact, proved to be more difficult than she anticipated. Despite her many criticisms of Douglas she has grown to rely on him and does not relish having to spend the evening either in the company of friends or by herself.

She is even feeling sentimental about their times together – which, she reflects, is positively ludicrous. The last time she saw him was Tuesday, when he walked off down the road, his straight black hair combed neatly as usual, his face pale with the effort of imposing a formality on their existing relationship.

'Well, don't pine without me,' was his parting remark, and immediately Paula's attitude towards him softened. His humour and generosity are the things about him she loves most, but they are all too often wiped out by his stiff reserve, his obsession with his career and a blind following of his parents' opinions.

It is this last feature that annoys Paula most, because she places such a high value on initiative and individual judgment. Moreover it seems to detract from his manliness. She simply cannot bear to see him regress into a little boy mentality when he is with his family.

Perhaps I'm just asking for the impossible, she thinks wryly, as she puts a final touch of polish to her writing table and rubs it vigorously with a cloth,

As she sits in front of the fire to read a book of poems by Lamartine, she has a sudden expansive feeling of autonomy and independence. She wonders whether it would be possible for her to be reasonably self-sufficient, with all her energies devoted to her career and her outside interests. The idea appeals to her and she considers its possibilities, as though turning over a flecked marble in different directions to catch the light. In some lights it seems tenable; in others impossible: the bonds she forms with people seem too strong, for even when she breaks them she does not feel free, but merely deserted.

Paula sighs. It seems ironic that she is single and has the hypothetical opportunity, because of her career and financial position, to be an independent career woman, but in practice cannot be so because of her temperament, whereas Alison, who is at present unqualified and involved in a failing marriage, could have grasped this opportunity with ease and fully relished it.

She is determined to enjoy this evening on her own and, to get herself into the right mood, puts an album by Theodorakis on her record player. The first two tracks are frisky dances, but she finds it difficult to enter fully into their mood and spirit; the third track is a recited poem, with an instrumental background played on the bouzouki. It tells of the Greek poet's travels through the world in soulful tones:

'Wherever I went, I encountered blood and tears,'

she hears, and suddenly overwhelmed with a desire to see Douglas again, Paula bursts into tears loudly on the settee. Immediately this is transformed into hysterical laughter as

119

she reflects on her own absurdity, sitting in the lamplit room, her hair still damp from washing it, and weeping over sentimental love songs.

21

A Common Female Trait

THE PHONE rings and June answers it.

'It's for you,' she says, handing it to Alison.

As Alison is talking, her face turns pale and her hands shake slightly.

'OK,' she says. 'Don't worry too much. Thanks for telling me. Bye.'

She puts down the phone and stands for a moment thinking, her forehead creased slightly, unsettling the smooth contours of her face.

'That was Dana,' she says eventually.

'What's the matter?' asks Paula, looking concerned.

'Margot's pregnant.'

'Oh.'

They all sit silent for a moment, their faces expressing a mixture of surprise and gradual acceptance.

'Well, I suppose it was to be expected at some point,' June says.

'Yes,' Alison says, her voice tight and clipped, 'but it's just bad luck that it should happen to her all the same. I mean, really it's a bloody nuisance under the circumstances. She's just started this project and Tony hasn't even finished his thesis and I think they have enough difficulty making ends meet as it is, what with Hilary, and also with Tony not working. Dana was telling me all about it the other day. Poor thing, she must be as worried as hell.'

'I can imagine,' Paula replies. 'I suppose I must be very immature, but I simply can't envisage wanting children at the moment – and as you know, it's been a bone of contention between me and Douglas – and of course with his parents as well. I don't know whether it's because I'm lacking in maternal feelings, or whether it's something hormonal, or simply that I'm too self-centred as a career woman to understand the ability to concern oneself continually with another human being.'

'That what you ought to be doing with Douglas,' Alison says wryly.

'I know I ought, but I think it's pretty obvious that I don't. For a start, he doesn't concern himself about me particularly. Oh well, I suppose I'm just—'

'It's a trend in present-day society,' William breaks in. 'The new liberated woman focuses her attention on herself.'

'Oh what a stupid generalisation,' Alison says angrily. 'You can't keep coming up with these platitudes. Everyone's an individual. There's no point in trying to sum everything up into one glib statement.'

William shakes his head, deciding it isn't worth getting into an argument with her in her present mood. Probably premenstrual, he decides, but wisely keeps the thought to himself.

'Anyway, now Dana's all worried at the thought of what she would do if she got pregnant,' Alison continues.

'Well, that's ridiculous – it's not infectious, you know,' June laughs.

'No, but it's put the idea into her head of how precarious her role in society is at present and—'

'I don't think it's precarious at all,' June says. 'She just happens to be living with Mike rather than being married to him because she doesn't want to be tied down by the formalities of marriage.'

'Well, I think in a way, she's just as tied down now as she would be if she were married,' Paula points out.

'I mean, she's completely dominated by Mike,' Alison says, 'though she pretends not to be. She always gives in to his opinions in the end. Still, we're digressing from the subject of Margot.'

'I suppose we shouldn't be gossiping for hours like this,' Paula says.

'Oh, it's a common female trait,' William says before he can stop himself.

They all burst out laughing.

'You're right there, William,' June says. 'It may be a generalisation but it's perfectly true. But what's wrong with a good old gossip – half the fun of having relationships is pulling them to pieces.'

'It's more fun pulling other people's relationships to pieces,' Alison laughs. 'It makes us feel superior.'

'It's not just that,' Paula says. 'I think one can genuinely see other people's situations much better than one's own.'

'Oh come off it,' Alison says. 'It may be enjoyable, but it's pretty pointless. Still, I suppose it's too late to change now.'

22

Naked Around the Corridors

DANA and Mike pause for a moment from sorting their books into different categories and burst out laughing. The situation really is ridiculous.

They have just moved into a new flat today, because the landlady of their former flat claimed to have seen Mike wandering naked around the corridors. Mike has denied it, though in his opinion there is no reason why he shouldn't wander naked around the corridors if he so chooses. However, he has put it down to the landlady's prurient imagination. Yet despite a long argument on the subject, the landlady has insisted on evicting them. She has 'generously' waived the monthly rent, provided they leave within a week, and fortunately they have found a much more spacious flat in the same area within a relatively short time of searching.

The main problem with this new flat, however, is that it is unfurnished and Mike has accumulated various odd pieces of furniture from local antique shops. Before they arrange their furniture and tidy up the flat, Mike has insisted on putting all the books into the three bookshelves and dusting each book. After an hour of dusting and sorting, they have only succeeded in filling one shelf and are surrounded by heaps of assorted books.

'God, I'm exhausted,' Dana says. 'I wish you wouldn't get these ridiculous ideas. Why can't we just bung the books into the shelves and sort them out later? This is so exhausting – and boring.'

'It'll save time in the long run. I'd rather we do the job properly now and not have to go over it all over again.'

'Why do I have to live with a perfectionist? I wouldn't mind if you were a perfectionist all the time, but you're not – only when it suits you.' She stands up, rubbing dust off her skirt. 'Anyway, I've had enough of this, I'm going to make some coffee.'

She walks past the bedroom – where cases and cartons are heaped over the double bed – to the kitchen, which looks onto the garden. Gazing out, Dana sees a young girl of about seventeen pegging washing out onto the line. The wind blows slightly, billowing the washing out into soft undulations and the girl's hair waves in the breeze.

Dana suddenly feels happy, and pleased with the move. It feels more peaceful here and much less suburban than their old flat. The kitchenette reminds her of a primitive country kitchen she once visited in Neuilly near Paris and all at once she has a warm, expansive sense of freedom: between them, she realises, they could make something original out of the flat, which reflects both of them – if only Mike could tear himself away from his work.

'Mike,' she shouts through to him. 'Come along out here at once!'

He appears at the door of the kitchen a moment later, a book in his hand.

'What's the matter?' he says anxiously. 'Are you all right?'

'Sure, I'm fine,' Dana laughs. 'I just wanted you to notice that I existed for a change, instead of being wrapped up in your cosy little world.'

'Oh is that all? I thought you'd had an accident or something. You gave me a shock. Don't do that again, for God's sake.'

'I'm glad I gave you a shock. It might at least shock you into life. I sometimes think you're like some kind of zombie, living in your books and articles and clever phrases... I'm me! I'm Dana! I'm here!'

'Don't be stupid,' he says dismissively.

'Why is that stupid? Isn't it important for us to speak to one another properly... for real? Why don't you ever say what you really mean? Why do you always talk around things? Why do you put on an act all the time?'

Mike sighs. 'What act? What are you talking about? There's nothing I particularly want to say to you at the moment. That's why I wasn't talking to you.'

Dana bursts into tears, 'You're cruel. If you've got nothing to say to me, I suppose I'm not worth talking to and we've got nothing to give each other.' She wipes a hand across her eyes, smudging the mascara with her tears. 'So why the bloody hell are we living together?' she screams. 'I must be stark, raving mad. Why am I still with you, you indifferent blob zombie, you nothing person!'

'You stick to me because you couldn't do without me,' he retorts smugly. 'And I don't suppose I could do without you, come to that – and I'm not indifferent to you. It's just that I'm busy. Look at the mess we're in. We must get this place straightened out.'

Dana starts to laugh in hysterical gasps. 'Oh my God, the way you get hold of an idea and then stick to it through thick and thin really curls me up.' She laughs again. 'I've never met anything like it. If it wasn't so horrible, it would be downright funny.'

Mike forces a laugh. 'I'm glad you're amused,' he says. 'Now stop being hysterical and come and help me with these books.

They walk back into the living room. Dana's face is vacant, as though she has been purged of her feelings and has nothing more to express.

23

Getting Back on Track

'ISN'T William back from lunch yet,' Alison says irritably. 'It's five past two.'

'You're getting as bad as Maggie,' Paula replies.

Alison frowns. 'Well, I think it's a bit—'

The door opens and William saunters in. 'Sorry, I'm late,' he says, 'I've just been to the library and was chatting to those women who are doing the project on the Duke of Bridchester. I think I've been able to give them an insight into the situation of the period from a sociological point of view.'

'Oh, how's Dana?' Alison asks. 'She's just moved, hasn't she?'

'She seems all right. I'm not that keen on her – she seems rather arrogant to me.'

Alison casts a knowing look at Paula.

'I like the little one – Anna,' he adds.

'Oh,' Alison says anxiously. 'You should be careful about getting involved with her – she's an in-patient at the Bridchester Infirmary.'

'No she's not. She's just come out. Apparently she's much better now and she's staying in a hostel down in Park Lane. Actually I think she's comparatively interesting compared to a lot of people. I've asked her out on Friday.'

Alison looks nervously at Paula. 'Do you think that's a good idea?' She is doing her best to be tactful.

'I'm not stupid, you know,' William snaps back angrily, 'or irresponsible for that matter. I did some psychology in my second term, actually. No, I just want to be friendly. We have a lot in common intellectually. I mean, if everyone leaves her alone, because she's so delicate and fragile mentally, she'll never get anywhere.'

Alison is obliged to agree with this, though she privately reflects that there are probably far more normal people Anna could meet than William, for whom by now Alison has formed an amused contempt. It then occurs to her that perhaps so-called normal people would not be interested in Anna.

'Well,' she relents, 'I think it's probably a good idea, as you say. Anyway, how has Dana settled down in her new flat?'

'Oh, apparently the place is fairly chaotic and they've still got a lot of unpacking to do. Dana sounds disgruntled by it all.'

Paula and Alison laugh heartily at this. 'Disgruntled is the perfect word to describe Dana,' Paula says. 'She always seems a little indignant about everything. Still, it's a good thing they moved when they did. It's not much fun living with a stroppy landlady. They used to live in Marshall Crescent, didn't they?'

'Yes,' Alison replies. 'I went round for coffee once. The flat was OK but the street was rather grotty.'

'Oh, well the new flat's in the same area,' William says.

'Typical. Dana's hopelessly disorganised. She just lets Mike do whatever he wants. It's really not fair and the annoying thing is that underneath, she always thinks he's right – I mean, he puts on an act of being a nice, decent bloke, and then he treats her as though she's inferior, because she's so high up in the clouds, but in fact she's quite original – a law unto herself and one of those people who really thinks about things.'

'Yes, I get the same impression,' Paula agrees, emerging from a cupboard with a pile of books. 'She tries to live according to her own rules, even if nobody agrees with them.'

'I think Anna's like that as well,' William says.

'No,' Alison says sharply, shaking her head. 'I don't think she ought to try too hard to think about things. It's more important for her to get on with her life – to get back on track.'

'*Get back on track!* What does that mean? Anyway, I think you underestimate her. Her attitude to history is really great.'

Alison sighs and exchanges a look with Paula.

'Here you are, William,' Paula says in a businesslike tone, handing him a box of envelopes and a sheaf of paper. 'If you wouldn't mind doing these envelopes for me. They're circulars for our next meeting.'

'What's it on?' Alison asks.

'Bridchester's agricultural history over the last five thousand years.'

'Delightful,' laughs June. 'I must remember to miss that one.'

'I don't know how you can say that,' William says. 'It could be interesting. Even if stuffing envelopes is soul-destroying, and hardly very remunerative. "Soul-destroying, but remunerative" – that's what my tutor always used to say to me about my vacation jobs before I dropped out.'

'Well, why don't you drop back in again,' Alison says sarcastically.

'Alison!' Paula reprimands her, anxious to keep the peace.

'No, I wasn't being bloody-minded,' Alison insists. 'I mean for the sake of your career. Don't you want a degree? You can't be satisfied about having left it in the middle.'

'I couldn't possibly finish a course that I felt to be intellectually shallow, irrelevant and outmoded,' William counters pompously. 'Besides which, after four months of freedom I don't think I'd get back into the routine particularly well.'

'Well, I hope you don't influence Anna the wrong way with your potty ideas,' Alison says bluntly.

'What do you mean potty—'

'Margot thinks she's capable of getting back to her studies pretty soon,' she continues, ignoring him,

'It was very nice of Margot to help her like that, wasn't it,' June says.

'I don't think Margot was trying to be nice,' Alison says. 'I don't even think she particularly likes Anna all that much. She just agreed to let her get involved because Anna showed an interest in it.'

'Well, Margot's going to have one more person to get involved in soon,' William points out.

'Yes... mind you, when I spoke to her on the phone yesterday about it, she sounded much more cheerful. She said it's going to be even more of a squeeze to make ends meet, but Tony is reconciled to the idea and they're quite happy about it now.'

'Sounds optimistic,' June says. 'I wish I could be like that.'

'When do you start your typing course?' William asks.

'September. And maybe I'll get to be somebody's PA.'

'Yes, your ambitions towards more and more self-exploitation know no bounds,' he says with a grin.

24

Anna and William
in the Rain

ANNA and William shiver from the rain as they enter the coffee-bar dripping wet and sit down at the table by the window. Anna hastily tries to wipe mud off her tights, which only serves to spread it in grey smears. William orders coffee and starts to expound on the novel he is writing.

'In a way I sympathise with your project,' he says, 'because compared with my writing, it's so tightly restricted. At the same time, you're lucky in that your subject is there and it's just a question of reaching out for it.'

'Well, what exactly are you trying to say in your novel?' Anna asks nervously, wondering whether William has overestimated his own intellectual abilities.

'My theme,' William replies with grandiosity, propping his thin elbows on the table and cupping his chin in one hand, 'is the central predicament of the twentieth century. We're living in a godless society and yet people are still searching for the truth – or rather, for truths. They're still religious, but they can't accept the old formulae. The family unit has disintegrated too.'

Anna winces at the sudden memory of an experience she had been suppressing for a long time.

'The old unit of mum and dad and two kids – this unit has vanished and people are reaching out for relationships with other parts of society. Nothing is certain or stable any more. Even our understanding of matter and energy has shifted. We think we know where everything is, but even the structure of the universe is not what we thought it was. According to quantum physics, particles can be in two places at once. Everything is uncertain and everything is fragmented.'

Anna smiles. William is expressing so easily and fluently ideas she has been trying to formulate.

'So life in this godless atmosphere is a nightmare,' William goes on. 'We are rudderless, we have no one to steer us, and we have to find some guidelines to help us get through it.'

'I've just been reading Kafka,' Anna says, putting a copy of *The Trial* on the table, 'and I'm feeling confused.'

William looks worried. 'I wouldn't try reading that at the moment. I read it quite a few years ago and I still remember the impression it left on me. I felt it was negative – it offered no positive belief or philosophy. It had no love or dynamism.'

'I think it has great compassion,' Anna says.

She sees him wince slightly and regrets that people don't like the fact that she is too direct and pointed, which they find embarrassing.

'But everything he says is very relevant in the political context of today,' William continues. 'I remember—'

The waitress has just brought them coffee and Anna has spilt some on her coat.

'I'd take that off if I were you,' William says. 'It looks as if it's soaked.'

'Yes, it is.' She pulls it off and rainwater streams onto the floor. Her hair, black and tangled, hangs on either side of her neck, almost meeting at the front.

'You're looking rather pre-Raphaelite today,' William says appreciatively.

'Thank you. I just feel very ordinary as usual.'

They lapse into silence and drink their coffee.

'How's the hostel?' he asks politely.

'It's OK. There's one woman – girl really – I don't like. She gets on my nerves. She keeps talking the whole time. One never has a moment's silence to think properly.'

'Oh you always get one person like that when you're living with other people. We had one at school, one at university—'

'Have you got one at your office? she asks curiously.

'No, not really. Mind you, I don't particularly like them. I find them all very artificial.' He immediately feels guilty and needs to qualifies this. 'But I suppose they're not so bad, and they're quite amusing to listen to. I mean, if you have to do a boring job, you might as well have some funny conversation to listen to, though most of it female gossip. Oh I'm sorry—'

But she doesn't seem to notice the hint of a sexist generalisation and instead says, 'Don't you prefer intelligent conversation to funny conversation?'

William reflects that Anna appears to be totally devoid of any sense of humour, which is a pity, because in other respects she appeals to him a lot.

'Not necessarily,' he replies, trying to summon up a friendly tone. 'It depends what mood I'm in. When I'm at work I tend to be rather lethargic, so I need bright superficial conversation to stimulate me, but in the evenings, when I'm alert anyway, I'm more in the mood to think deeply about things.'

'I wish I could,' Anna says sadly.

'Could what?'

'Think deeply, I do try sometimes, but it doesn't seem to get me anywhere. It's as much as I can do to get on with things.'

William relaxes and smiles warmly at her. 'I expect it will come in time. Anyway, at least you do try, and you're aware of it all. Some people are just half-asleep, zombies – look at them,' he adds contemptuously, as a group of giggling teenagers run past the café windows, eating hot dogs and shouting.

'We don't know anything about them,' Anna says thoughtfully. 'Oh well, if I give up Kafka for the moment, who would you recommend as an alternative?'

'How about Thomas Hardy?' William suggests. 'Wholesome, lyrical, readable, poetic?'

Anna groans and William decides that perhaps she does have a sense of humour after all.

'Yes and tragic – I don't think I can cope with that at the moment. I tried reading him a few months ago and it made me feel even worse.'

She stares solemnly at the crowded street outside with figures moving through the rain and her breath blows steamy patches against the window, muffling the view. It seems to her that this misty barrier is like her own illness, coming between herself and other people – even those who try to defend her.

William also stares silently at the world outside and wonders whether to ask her to a party next Saturday. It will be a fairly simple affair and he doesn't have a girlfriend to take. He looks at her serious, solemn face a little dubiously and ponders for a moment before deciding.

25

Party Night

'HERE we are,' William says, pulling his battered old green Mini to a halt in a dark lane outside a lighted window. 'This must be it,'

Anne stares apprehensively at the red lamp which glows through the front living room and the dark figures of mainly young men and women who seem to be loping from side to side, holding glasses of wine, sherry, beer or fruit punch.

'Oh, it must be. There aren't any other lights for miles.'

'Pete's too lazy to clear away all these weeds,' he says as they walk down the dark garden path.

Pete, the host, is William's former tutor and now one of his closest friends – or so William has informed Anne. But when they enter, Pete scarcely seems to recognise him. However, he politely escorts them through the crowd in the doorway, introducing them to various people.

Yesterday Anne had her hair restyled, layered and sculpted and the effect, if not pretty or glamorous, is definitely interesting, accentuating the dark intensity of her eyes. She looks nervously around at the group dancing in the dimly lit back room.

A small woman in a white dress emerged and recognises her.

'Hello, Anna,' she says in surprise.

'Hello, Jenny,' Anna replies a little nervously.

'Are you... I mean, how lovely to see you again. This is terrific. Come along in.'

She drags Anna into the centre of the room and Anna nearly crashes into a gyrating couple,

Jennifer Ellis is a third-year mathematics student and was a frequent visitor to the Infirmary during Anna's first few weeks there, but her visits have tailed off recently due to the pressure of revision.

Anna looks round, realising that William has disappeared, and catches a glimpse of him talking to a friend in the corridor, but they seem to be involved in a heated discussion. Jenny has meanwhile dragged her fiancé in to meet Anna.

'John, you remember Anna Crawley,' she says, her face expressing friendliness mixed with significant warning.

'Yes, of course,' he replies warmly and stares at Anna in evident surprise. 'God, you look terrific – you look completely different. I don't know what it is about you.'

'It's her hair,' Jenny says. 'And you're figure looks better, Anna. You've put on weight – it suits you much better.'

Several other people Anna vaguely knows drift up and join in the general fluttering of surprise at her appearance. At first she can't decide whether they are merely being polite or whether they are actually pleased to see her in circulation again, but after a few seconds of anxious speculation, she decides to relax and begins to dance with a tall, thin bearded man.

As the music changes to a slow dance, she suddenly finds herself being held very closely in a surprisingly strong grip, At first Anna quite enjoys this but starts to become aware that he is pressing his body against her – and his beard is uncom-

fortably prickling against her forehead – and when he begins
muttering suggestions into her ear, she yanks herself out of
his grasp and rushes out into the other room to find William.

He is squatting in a corner, surrounded by a half-circle of
listeners, to whom he is expounding on his usual themes.

'William,' Anna says, rushing towards him gratefully,
suddenly regarding him as an old friend, someone she knows
and can trust, surrounded as she is by a crowd of strangers.
William pauses in mid-sentence, his mouth dropping open.

'God, I'd forgotten about you. Are you all right?'

'Yes, of course.' Uncharacteristically, she giggles.

'Are you having a good time?'

'Well, yes and no,' she says. 'It's not… I mean, there's no
intellectual stimulus. I was dancing with that man over there,
the tall one with the beard.'

Everybody laughs and Anna, who has had no intention of
being amusing, feels compelled to continue her train of intro-
spective thought – which is quite normal to her – in order to
amuse them.

'There a contrast,' she says, 'between the levity of the
music and the gloom which descends on me as I see these
shadowy figures.'

They all laugh again and one woman even gets hiccups.
'William's blarney is obviously contagious,' she splutters.

William looks up and motions Anna to be quiet, saying,
'Let's get back to my original hypothesis.'

'I'd much rather listen to this young lady,' Arnold says –
a plump man wearing owlish glasses and a black sweater –
who is a friend of Pete's. 'I like her complete lack of inhibi-
tion – as though she is free to voice whatever arises in the

narrative stream of her subconscious intellect – or to put it another way, Woolf and Joyce's stream of consciousness...'

'Well, that's not really natural for me. It's the result of—'

'Anna,' William interrupts. 'Have some of this cheese – it's fantastic.'

'I'm not allowed to eat cheese,' Anna replies in a high, clear voice.

The laughter finally dies down and the hiccupping woman passes Anna a cushion to sit on.

'As I was saying,' William continues, 'people are getting away for the first time from the rigid institutionalism to which they have always been subjected. First it was the kindergarten, then school, then university, then some professional environment such as the law courts or hospitals or civil service, but for most it meant some dreary office—'

'Well, who asked you to go and work in a dreary office?' the fat man says.

'Nobody, Arnold. I did it as an act of subversion – to infiltrate the institutions of bureaucracy at the workplace level and to undermine those in service to institutionalism—'

'But didn't you just say that institutionalism was dying out?' Arnold says. 'Honestly, it's impossible to have a straight conversation if you keep contradicting yourself.'

'I'm *not* having a conversation,' William shouts. 'I'm giving you my ideas – I'm delivering a monologue. This is a William-session, not a free-for-all debate.'

'Well, I've had enough of William sessions. It was bad enough when you were actually studying all this rubbish, but now that you've dropped out of it, your ideas are getting illogical – in fact, they're positively cranky.'

'It's very easy to label ideas you don't agree with as cranky. In fact, it's an excuse for not opening your mind to new possibilities. It's so facile to stick to the old, run-of-the-mill arguments and —'

At this point, Arnold stuffs a very big meringue into William's opened mouth, and everybody roars.

'That's terrific,' Miss Hiccups says. 'You're a real goon tonight, William. You'd make a marvellous clown.' She stands up, still hiccupping, and begins pirouetting around the room, singing 'I'm Coco the Clown, I am, I am…'

'She's had a bit too much cider,' Arnold says. 'Have a meringue, love,' he adds, passing the plate to Anna. 'I trust you're allowed to eat these?'

'Yes, thank you,' she replies and picking out a large meringue, nibbles it delicately in an impossible attempt to eat one grain of sugar at a time.

'Are you all right?' William asks, moving up to Anna and putting an arm round her. 'You look like my favourite holiday pony nibbling its lump of sugar.'

'Show a few more manners towards that young lady,' Arnold says.

'Oh, go and jump out of the window, you stuffed owl,' William says. 'I'm sick of you and your pointless quips and interruptions.'

'My pointless quips and interruptions?' Arnold mocks, and the group all laugh again. 'What you call pointless quips and interruptions is what most reasonable people would call having a sensible discussion and sometimes it's best to remain silent.'

Just as he says this the record ends and everyone sits in embarrassed silence, waiting for the next record to begin.

'What's happened to the bloody record player!' Arnold says, contradicting his own call to silence, just as Jenny comes into the room carrying a pile of 45s and hands them to a lean, bespectacled young man standing forlornly by the record player.

'These are more fun,' she says and kneels down beside Anna, just as a small, white kitten wriggles out from under the table. Anna lifts it onto her lap. As the kitten begins to mew in protest, a record blares out very loudly, shattering the silence – and it is finally too much for Anna.

'I'm going home,' she mutters to William and rushes out of the room, grabbing her coat and running down the lane, through the streets and back to her hostel, as William sits staring nonchalantly into thin air trying to hide the mixture of guilt he is feeling about Anna and acute embarrassment at his own humiliation at the hands of Arnold.

26

The Theologist

A S PAULA enters the town hall, she is feeling reluctant and half-hearted about even being there. She has to help prepare one of the lecture rooms for the meeting but has neither the inclination to attend a meeting of any sort this evening, nor any wish to hear about the religious hierarchy of thirteenth-century Bridchester.

She starts putting out chairs in rows when she hears a banging sound behind the left door, which opens to reveal a young man carrying a large projector screen into the room. He is stocky, with a balding head, large black spectacles, and the face of a tired academic, pale and drawn into concentrated scrutiny of the hall. He deftly adjusts the screen and walks into an adjacent room.

Paula, realising that her eyes have grown accustomed to the gloom, switches on all the lights and as she starts placing leaflets on the chairs, she hears Miss Bushnell greeting the man in the next room with effervescent politeness.

'How very nice of you to come so promptly, Roger. I always think it's so much wiser to get settled properly before one has to speak. Of course, I've had quite a lot of experience of it myself. You see…'

She marches briskly into the hall, her expression changing from formal politeness to authority.

'Ah, Paula. Will you tell Mr Enright something about our society. I've got so many things to organise. I really don't know where to begin.'

She carries on talking as she marches out of the room, high heels clicking assertively along the wooden corridor. Paula, feeling sullen and tired, says brusquely to Roger, 'Well, what do you want to know?'

'Nothing. I'm pleased enough to get in out of the rain. It's a dismal night, isn't it.' He rubs his hands energetically. 'Still, I hope a few people will turn up. I like company. I don't want to have to talk all on my own.'

Paula detects a sadness behind his affectation of geniality and humour. This endears him to her, for she herself always affects a poker-faced nonchalance when meeting people for the first time.

'Oh yes,' she replies, 'we'll probably get an enormous turnout. The second-year history students are very keen on this society.'

'You don't sound too keen yourself,' he laughs.

'Well, I haven't got anything against it in theory, but it's sort of been thrust upon me, so I'm feeling somewhat semi-detached about the whole idea.'

He glances at the next room where Miss Bushnell is talking loudly on the phone, and smiles. Paula realises that his humour is not an affectation – it arises more from a sense of irony than of cheerfulness. At the same moment it occurs to her that she likes him and as soon as this thought strikes her, she finds herself unable to think of anything to say. He looks inquisitively at her for a moment with a curious openness, then a polite mask seems to descend over his face.

'I quite enjoy giving these outside lectures, actually. It's a change from academic work.'

'Well, I'd better warn you that you'll meet lots of old dears and eccentric bods tonight,' Paula says, recovering her composure. 'That's one interesting side of it.'

'Oh, you like meeting curious characters, do you?' he asks jovially.

'Not particularly, but they're one degree more interesting than stuffy academics.'

'I take it you're not a stuffy academic yourself,' he smiles.

'Well, I read history at Cambridge, but that hardly qualifies, and then—'

She stops abruptly, annoyed that his face has taken on a respectful expression and disliking herself for unintentional boasting. 'Oh and then I studied archive management and now I'm at the Records Office.'

'Really? That's a coincidence. My brother's an archivist as well.'

Paula thinks with mild irritation that it's hardly a huge coincidence. She smiles and asks formally, 'And what about you?'

'Oh, I lecture in theology.'

'Do you? How funny. I mean, I assumed your subject was history.'

'Why?'

'I don't know – I just did.'

Paula feels a mixture of fatigue and embarrassment and they sit in silence for a long moment until Roger's face is suddenly restored to life.

'Well, I'd better prepare my slides. I expect the epidia-scope will conk out halfway through. These wretched things usually do.'

Paula senses that the hearty manner he has adopted is unnatural to him, but she is grateful for the attempt as it pre-cludes much effort on her part; she continues to distribute leaflets on the chairs just as Miss Bushnell returns.

'Paula,' she exclaims, 'I do think it's dreadful. Do you remember that woman who gatecrashed our opening recep-tion – you know, Professor Newsom's daughter?'

'Oh, er... yes?'

'Well, apparently she's now involved in some research project into one of the dukes of Bridchester and she's actually asked for the searchroom hours to be extended. I do think she's got a cheek. That type of person always takes advantage of the facilities offered. I told her father on the phone just now that if she's that keen on the project, then she should fit in with our hours. I mean, we can't make exemptions for one person.'

'Quite.'

'No, it's not even as if she were anybody. I don't know, perhaps I'm just getting old-fashioned, but it seems to me that some of these people have really had everything much too soft.'

Miss Bushnell walks up to the other end of the room and repositions the vases of flowers on the table with noisy exacti-tude.

'When I was in my teens I had a terribly hard time.'

Paula is on the point of saying, *I don't think she's in her teens*, when she decides it would be more diplomatic to conceal her friendship with Dana and, hating herself for her hypocrisy, she smiles instead and says, 'I understand.'

'Good. I'm glad someone does. Come along,' she adds to Roger, 'I'll make you some coffee before the meeting. And you can join us, Paula.'

27

History Class

ACH of the twelve students in Alison's history class has to read a short essay on the Reformation and she is feeling apprehensive Her own piece was written hurriedly last night, with little planning or forethought and with even less success, and although it's adequate it is obviously unoriginal and spiritless.

The last student to read sits down nervously at the front of the class. She is thin with broad shoulders, a colourless face and long brown hair. As she reads, she turns the sleeves of her baggy sweater up to her elbows and twiddles with the ends of her hair. Her essay is succinct and carefully structured and expressed. Each phrase surprises the ear by its originality and Alison's attention is gripped and drawn through a long, convoluted path of ideas, which finally come to a logical conclusion.

'I'm not sure about the ending,' comments Pete Matthews. 'It's a little too obvious, but as for the rest… What did you all think of it?'

'Excellent,' Andrew says, a dour Scot in his forties, who normally adopts a deeply critical tone.

'And what about you, Jean?' Pete asks.

A small woman with elfin features and hairstyle, Jean screws up her eyes intensely and speaks with a defect in her 'r's, though each word is carefully intonated, so that the effect is songlike rather than conversational.

'I felt that it was the only essay that was in any way diffewent from the pedestwian, wun-of-the-mill standard of the others. Apart from the details behind the study, there was a pwecision of thought and logic in the exposition, which made it both easy to follow, yet difficult – in the best sense of the word – and stimulating to gwasp, because of the subtlety of the ideas.'

'I see,' Pete says. 'Well expw— expressed. Yes, I know what you mean. What did you think, Alison?'

'Well, it was very good, original, clear and stimulating.'

'Yes, and what was it about it that made it different, for instance, from your own work? Can you define the quality?'

Alison blushes, and blinks as a few wisps of hair fall into her eyes.

'It has a quality of enthusiasm,' she says carefully.

'Precisely. I think the trouble with this class is that you're just not putting enough into it... You've got to stretch yourselves to the full limit. You've got to use your mind and your imagination, not just churn out the same second-rate ideas you've found in some text book. Think of what it's like for me, having to criticise the stuff. Put yourself in my position, I've heard it all before, many times. What I need is a new angle, something beautiful, something with fire in it.'

'It's very difficult getting back to study after a day at work,' Alison says, feeling a mixture of jealousy for the best student and gratitude to Pete for not pulling his punches – for speaking honestly and directly and helping them to understand their weaknesses.'

'Time – I understand. However,' he thumps the table loudly and they all laugh, partly out of shock, 'you won't listen to a word I say and you'll all go home and do exactly the same thing next week. I know.'

They all laugh again and Alison suddenly loses her temper, her nerves exacerbated by mental exhaustion and frustration at being unable to achieve the standards he demands.

'I'm sorry but I just want to pass my bloody exams. I don't care two hoots what so-called scholastic standards I achieve.'

She throws her books in her bag and rushes out of the room, slamming the door and just looking round in time to savour the rows of surprised eyes gazing at her with a mixture of embarrassment and amusement.

As soon as she has left the university building, she regrets her outburst. Not only will Pete be angry, but it will be difficult to re-adopt the social veneer required at such classes. Moreover the others will label her as hysterical, unstable and out of control. However, despite these misgivings, she feels oddly relieved by her outburst.

She knows that she can be like a pressure cooker, prone to building up feelings of violent anger which sometimes require hysterical release for her to regain a state of equilibrium, and as she walks through the streets of Bridchester she can now enjoy the crisp late afternoon sunshine and other people's flickering shadows, the movement of light on the pavements, for her gaze is directed downwards, as it always is when she is deep in thought.

A Tonibell ice-cream van plays its tune as it passes her and stops at the corner. She rushes up to buy a large double cornet, which she eats greedily as she walks past the parade of shops in the centre of town, dodging to avoid fellow pedestrians – and at the thought of the word 'pedestrians' her heart sinks. Her work has been labelled 'pedestrian', but it is not that fact that annoys her, for she has been aware of this for some time. It is rather her inability to be content with academic ability.

She has no academic aspirations, yet she feels so dissatisfied that her own abilities are limited. Mingled with this feeling is the commonsense knowledge that she should learn to accept herself and face her personality as it is, rather than continually wanting to be what she is not.

Just as she is deep in these thoughts, someone says 'hello', and looking up she sees Anna Crawley, smiling timidly at her. They met last week at a talk on the religious hierarchy of medieval Bridchester.

'Hello,' Alison says, smiling warmly. 'What a lovely day.'

'Yes, isn't it. I've just been buying clothes in Marks and Sparks.'

'Oh, what did you get?'

'This and this,' Anna says, lifting out a pink and mauve ribbed jumper and a purple skirt from her carrier bag.

'Oh, they're super. Really fantastic. Gosh, I wish I was slim like you, you lucky thing.'

'Yes... I must go,' Anna says awkwardly. 'I've got to see someone.'

'OK,' Alison says. 'See you.'

She continues her walk briskly down the road and then, forgetting all her academic problems, decides to go and see an Italian movie at the local arts cinema.

28

Pushing a Pram

MARGOT walks slowly out into the dazzling sunshine of the back garden where Hilary is playing with her four-year-old friend Sally from next door. They are pushing a small pram round the lawn, but when Margot approaches she sees that they're not playing but squabbling – or rather, Hilary is being bossy.

'Go away Sally,' she says grumpily. 'Go away. I don't want to play with you today.'

'Why not?' Sally replies indignantly, her eyes instantly filling with tears.

'Because you're in the way and I can't push the pram round the garden prop'ly if your hands are in the way. You can sit down over there and watch me.'

'All right,' Sally says submissively – to Margot's surprise.

Margot puts up a deckchair and gets out her knitting.

'What are you knitting, Margot?' Sally asks.

'You shouldn't call her Margot,' Hilary rebukes her. 'She's not Margot, she's my Mummy.'

'But she's not *my* mummy. She's Margot.'

Hilary, floored by this logic, stares open-mouthed at Sally for a moment, and then makes revving engine noises – 'brrrng, brrrng, brrrng' – as she pushes the pram even more vigorously in circles round and round a small area of grass.

'You'll get dizzy doing that, Hilary,' Margot says, looking up momentarily from her knitting.

'But I like being dizzy – it's nice,' Hilary says. 'Mummy, what are you knitting?'

'A pullover for Daddy,' Margot replies, flicking a ball of red wool along the grass so that it gradually moves closer to her.

'Why don't you buy one for him? Why do you knit it?' Sally asks.

'So that I can choose the colour and style I want.'

'Yes,' Hilary says, 'and Mummy made me a cargidan in my fav'rite colour. It was green and blue.'

'I don't like blue,' Sally declares, 'but I do like green.' She twirls round in the grass. 'Green, green, green.' Then she skips over to the pram, which Hilary has now abandoned, and runs down the garden with it, singing 'Green, green, green.'

'Oh Sally.' Hilary squeals, 'you're a very, very naughty girl. You've taken my pram and I didn't say you could.'

'Hilary, you mustn't keep bossing Sally around all the time,' Margot reprimands her.

By this time Sally has reappeared, gurgling with laughter.

'But I *can* boss Sally around, Mummy,' Hilary says, 'because she's much, much younger than me. She's only four and a quarter and I'm four and a half.'

'Yes, but soon I'll be four and a half and then I'll be as old as you.'

'You won't, you won't,' Hilary shouts, 'because I'll be even older than you, I'll be…'

She tries to work out the sum on her fingers, and then gives up, stamping her foot crossly. 'Anyway, if I tell you to obey me, you must obey me.'

At this point the phone rings and Margot runs off into the kitchen, clutching her stomach as she feels a downward lurching of sickness, and picks up the phone.

'Hi,' Dana says. 'I've had some inspiration about it.'

Margot immediately understands 'it' to be the Duke of Bridchester project. 'Really?'

'Yes, but it's really too complicated to tell you over the phone. Can I pop over to discuss it with you?'

'Sure,' Margot says, 'I'm having a totally lazy afternoon, basking in the sun and playing with the children.'

'Children?' Dana repeats apprehensively.

Margot, remembering that Dana has an aversion to children, adds diplomatically, 'Actually, they're due for a nap soon. They should have had it an hour ago, but it was such a gorgeous day, I wanted them to get some fresh air and they'll probably rest better after all that exercise.'

'Sure,' Dana says. 'I'm a sun-worshipper as well, Mike's always telling me I must have been an Ancient Egyptian in one of my former existences.'

'One of them?' Margot asks curiously.

'Yes. Not only am I a hopeless layabout but I believe in the transmigration of souls. However, that's too vast a subject to discuss over the phone.'

'Sure is!' Margot laughs.

'So I'll see you in about half an hour. Goodbye.'

'Bye, Dana.'

In a few minutes Margot has deftly tidied the living room and kitchen. She walks sleepily back into the garden. Sunshine always has a soporific effect on her and she sits down for a ten-minute nap before putting the children to bed.

She lies back in the sunshine, kaleidoscopic patterns forming in multicoloured dots behind the blackness of her eyelids, the voices of the squabbling children leaping into her half-dreaming state, like sparks fizzing out of a fire into the grate, and as she dozes she feels a tremendous sense of tranquillity, as though her life, though disorganised and problematic, has stretched itself into branches in different directions and even in her very different relationships with her husband and daughter and friends, she feels herself extended and fulfilled...

29

Bench Talk

'NEED some red cabbage for a new recipe I'm cooking to-morrow,' Alison says as she and Paula walk through the high street.

'Oh?'

Alison gives her an odd look. 'You're in a very funny mood today. What's up?'

Paula blushes but says nothing.

'Is it something to do with Douglas?' Alison asks, swerving to avoid two women with baby buggies who were about to run her down.

'Indirectly,' Paula sighs.

Alison stops by a lamppost and pushing Paula to a standstill out of the mainstream of pedestrians, she prepares for a showdown.

'Well, what is it? Out with it! You've been acting oddly all week.'

Paula sighs again. 'I've got a problem – look, we can't talk here, let's go into the square and sit down.'

They make their way to a group of benches arranged around a fountain in the middle of the square and seat themselves on the one empty bench. Alison takes out a packet of Woodbines and lights one.

'I know, I shouldn't smoke – you needn't tell me – but I expect my lungs are pretty reedlike already. As far as your problem is concerned,' she blows a small ring of smoke, 'it's obvious you're dead sick of Douglas and my guess is you've met someone else and are in love with them, so the solution is – well, chuck Doug and go out with the new bloke.'

Paula stares wide-eyed at Alison, her pupils dilated with surprise, eyes dark grey against her pale complexion.

'How on earth did you know?' Her face is suffused a blotchy pink. 'God, I didn't know I was so transparent!'

Alison laughs. 'Well, you're not usually, but I think I know you well enough to guess the truth in this case. So anyway, what's the problem?'

Paula blushes again. 'Actually, it's rather embarrassing. You see, I hardly know him, so I can't really call it "love". It's probably just infatuation. In fact, I feel thoroughly adolescent about it. Sometimes I feel so miserable I just sit and cry because I begin to wonder whether I even know what my own feelings are, and I'm sure he doesn't give me a thought.'

She blushes an even darker shade of pink. 'Actually, I've only met him twice.'

Alison stares with incredulity at Paula, who is normally so poised and calm.

'Well, there's no need to get so worked up about it. Either he does like you or he doesn't and if he doesn't, you can just drop the idea of him. You said yourself you hardly known him. I don't see what you're so upset about.'

Paula laughs. 'Put like that, it does sound trivial. But one doesn't think logically in these cases. One's mind just keeps rolling round and round, churning with the same hopes and—'

Alison smiles. 'Good God. You sound like something out of *Woman's Own*.'

Paula kicks a leaf on the ground angrily with her shoe. 'That's the trouble with us, Alison. We think we're too cultured, too sophisticated. As soon as any genuine emotion comes along, we're embarrassed and make a joke about it. Why can't you be simple? Why can't you be natural?... I'm terribly in love,' she finishes quietly.

Alison's face suddenly grows serious. 'Who with?'

Paula gulps and stiffens slightly. 'Roger.'

'Who?' Alison screws up her face in an effort to recall the name.

'Roger Enright – you know, the lecturer the other month, at the society. Oh, I know you'll laugh. I hardly knew him and he looks so ordinary but I can't help it. It may be silly, but I've never felt like this before.'

Alison looks sympathetically at Paula. 'I'm sorry, I'm not laughing or criticising. I understand.'

Paula snorts. 'I'm sure you don't. I mean, he looks an absolute nothing, but—'

'It's not a question of looks in these matters,' Alison sighs.

'Well, we went out for a drink after the meeting and talked and ... I just realised he was fantastic. It wasn't so much him. It was more the fact that we got on so well together.'

Alison laughs. 'Now that's going a bit far. Of course it was him. You're absolutely crazy about him.'

'But Alison, I hardly know him. The second time I saw him was when I met him in Queen Street last Tuesday and he asked me round to supper.' She scuffs the leaf again with her shoe. 'And I bloody well said no, because I thought I wanted to give it another go with Douglas, but now I know I don't and it's too late.'

'But Paula, that's fantastic. If he actually asked you out, he's obviously interested in seeing you again – or at the very least, is aware you exist. The way you put it before, I assumed the whole thing was in your imagination.'

'But a casual invitation to supper. He's probably invited hundreds of women to supper. I just don't know what to do.'

Alison crosses her legs, smooths her hair away from her face, and leaning down, stubs out her cigarette on the ground. 'Well, to be honest, I think you're making a mountain out of a molehill. Just give it a few days to simmer down in your mind and then if you still feel the same way about him, get back in touch. I mean, it shouldn't be too hard to find him – we've got all the directories at your disposal.'

Paula visualises the shelf of directories and lists of university lecturers at the back of her office. They suddenly seem comforting, full of promise, and hope for the future.

30

Writers' Club

'Now don't be shy, whatever happens,' William tells Anna as they wait outside the door of the flat where his writers' club meeting is being held. 'Just be yourself. Talk to them in the same way you talk to me.'

'It's so difficult.'

William looks down at her irritably, then his face breaks into a grin. 'Oh well,' he says, 'there are loads of neurotics at this club. I think most people who write are neurotic in some way.'

Anna is quietly appalled at William's complete unawareness of what her mental condition might be and his ignorant labelling of it as 'neurotic' but says nothing as the door opens and a tall woman with grey hair pinned up into an untidy bun ushers them in.

'I heard that remark,' she says sternly. 'What an enormous generalisation. I didn't think you were capable of such platitudes, William.'

'Well, I'm not usually,' he laughs. 'Only when I'm in the right mood. Madeleine, this is Anna.'

Anna walks timidly into the living room where the meeting is taking place. It is small and rectangular, filled with grey chairs, sofas and window-seats. The room is crowded with people.

'Do have a seat, Anna,' Madeleine says, leading her to a wooden chair in the corner.

William sits down informally at her feet and Anna begins to relax, overhearing snatches of conversation.

'Right in the middle of my bath, of all the bloody cheek...'

'Well, what can you expect if they import them from Spain...'

'So the inevitable result is an impasse on all sides...'

'I think the name Madeleine suits her,' Anna whispers to William and glancing at their hostess.

'Do you think so?'

'Yes, she has a sort of regal air about her.'

William adjusts his legs and rests his elbow against the ledge of Anna's chair. 'I always think of the name Madeleine as belonging to a woman in a fashion parade, so I suppose it does suit her for that reason.'

'That seems a very 1950s-ish thing to say,' Anna laughs.

He looks up at her: these days she seems considerably more normal, as he terms it to himself.

'I've been writing a lot of poems over the past few days,' Anna tells him. 'They're in the form of a cycle. Actually they were inspired by the death of the Duke of Bridchester. The idea came to me while I was writing up the details for Margot.'

'Margot's an odd person,' William says. 'She's very kind and very nice and I feel I ought to like her, but for some reason I don't.'

'Maybe she's not your type and vice versa.'

William winces at this jargon, which sounds so unnatural, coming as it does from Anna. He pauses for a moment and assuming what he thinks is a roguish countenance, says, 'So don't I inspire you with romantic feelings?'

'No.'

William is stung by the flatness of her reply. 'Not even a little?' he perseveres.

'No, you're a nice person, but at the moment I don't feel like loving anybody else.'

'Anybody else?' William wonders fleetingly whether she has been jilted by someone, or whether an unhappy love affair was the reason for her breakdown.

'Anybody else apart from myself,' Anna explains. 'It's difficult enough to do that.'

A man sitting nearby smiles. 'What a glorious way of putting it. I'll have to put that in my novel.'

'But Anna,' William continues, ignoring the interruption. 'Sometimes I think that... I actually love you.' He blushes with embarrassment.

Anna stares solemnly at his small white face, perched on top of his small frame, and at his long, straggly blond hair, which hangs forlornly around his shoulders.

'Oh William,' she says, 'I'm very flattered, but you don't really know me. You're just sorry for me because of my breakdown and maybe you're projecting something on to me. Anyway I feel that once I recover fully and become myself again, we won't have much in common.'

'But what do you mean by "myself"? What is yourself, Anna?' he asks, knowing that he is treading on dangerous ground with this line of questioning, but barging on nevertheless.

At this moment, Madeleine comes over to him and sitting on a pouffe, her plaited skirt neatly covering her knees, she asks William, 'Tell me, why do you write? Is it because there's something you want to express that you can't do in conversation, or is it because you want to have contact with the Other?'

'Both,' William says curtly, still stinging from Anna's rebuff.

'Isn't it odd,' Anna says, 'that some people don't feel this same need to make complete contact. I mean, they just make some kind of partial contact through conversation, and there are whole areas of their minds and consciousness that remain unexplored and unexpressed, but it doesn't seem to matter to them.'

'Exactly,' Madeleine says, frowning earnestly, 'but what is it that motivates some people to want to make that complete kind of contact and not others?'

'Who knows?' William says. 'The true nature of human consciousness is one of the three most difficult problems in life, and you can't sum them up in a few words.'

'Oh yes, I do agree,' Madeleine replies. 'So what in your opinion are the other two most difficult problems in life?'

'Whether God exists and the meaning of suffering,' William says, a touch too glibly.

'Don't make a mockery of such things,' Anna says.

'It reminds me a little of Professor Newsom the way you say that,' Madeleine says. 'He always comes out with the most extraordinarily insightful comments, which he delivers without batting an eyelid. I can never understand how he does it.'

'Practice makes perfect. I swear at myself every day in front of the mirror without batting an eyelid. It's an enormous strain on the eye muscles, but it does my sang-froid the world of good.'

'Oh William,' Anna sighs, 'I wish you didn't talk such a lot of rubbish.' She glances across at the doorway. 'Look who's just walked in.'

She smiles tentatively as Dana walks over to greet her.

'Hi, Anna,' she says warmly. 'Hi, William,' she adds, her voice hardening a shade. 'Anna. I've just written a load of garbage, and I'm now about to inflict it on the assembled company.'

'It can't be as bad as my poem cycle,' Anna replies.

As she speaks, Madeleine claps her hands, there's a general hush, and the meeting commences.

31

A Most Peculiar Relationship

ALISON rushes into the office, where Paula is sitting over a pile of books.

'Dana's coming round in a minute,' she says anxiously. 'I met her in the high street and she looked just like death warmed up. I can't think what the hell's up with her. She looked really awful. I suppose it was because she wasn't wearing any make-up and her hair was tied straight back.'

'It may be some trouble with Mike. I heard them arguing the last time they were at a society meeting together. There seems to be a total lack of communication between them. To tell you the truth, I felt more sorry for Mike than for her. She's so cold to him sometimes.'

'Oh, I think he's pretty thick-skinned,' Alison replies. 'I mean they both are. They really have a most peculiar relationship—'

Just as she says this, the door opens and Dana walks in. Paula blushes and Alison sits down guiltily.

'I heard that,' Dana says sourly. 'Well, you're right – we do have *a most peculiar relationship*... no, you're wrong – we don't have one at all any more.'

She sits down on a chair by the window and laughs hysterically.

'Oh God, Dana, are you all right?' Alison asks.

'Sure. I'll be just fine in a moment. I'm just feeling so relieved. I'm so glad to be through with Mike. It's like at long last we've broken down all those fences and can tell each other just how much we don't give a damn about each other.'

'But you don't, Dana – you love each other really,' Alison insists.

'We don't love each other and we're not in love – we're in hate, except that's too good a word for it. We feel nothing for each other any more – we're just sick of each other. That just about sums up how stale our non-relationship is. It's just been dragging on and on—'

'What happened?' Alison breaks in.

'Well, to start with, I'm very homesick, and I want to go back home. So I told him about it and he just laughed and said it would wear off. That's how much he cares for me. And secondly, he's been seeing another woman.'

'But I thought you didn't believe in exclusive relationships,' Paula says.

'Well, I certainly don't believe in the sacredness of marriage. But I don't bloody well want Mike going off with someone else while I'm living with him.'

'It's a bit of a nerve,' Alison says.

'*A nerve!*' Dana shrieks. 'I was so goddamned furious I nearly threw away all his notes for his latest article, and then I kind of melted. I mean, I could murder him quite easily, but somehow I couldn't bring myself to destroy his work.' She laughs.

'Oh Dana, how can you sit there and laugh like this? It's all so terrible,' Alison says.

'What's terrible? I feel free and happy and I'm going back home. I'm so homesick. I want to see my mother and my family and friends in Ontario again. I've enjoyed Bridchester – I've got a big kick out of being here and it's really stretched me – you know it did – but somehow I'm feeling kind of restless, and to be honest, I've got my eye on someone back home, who's just written me a very friendly letter.'

'I thought as much,' Alison says. 'I guessed there might be someone else.'

'Oh, what the hell.' Dana stretches out her arms and stands up, gyrating a few steps across the room.

'You look like Isadora Duncan gone wrong,' says William, who has been quietly listening all this time.

'Thanks a lot. I may be hopeless and amoral, but at least I can dance.'

'What about your research project?' Paula asks. 'Margot and Anna will be disappointed.'

'Well, Margot's pregnant so she's taking a back seat, but as Anna seems to be much better now, I've asked her if she might consider taking the project over. We'll see, and if she's not up to it… well, it may have to go by the board. It's a pity, but there it is.'

'Oh, I don't mind taking your place on the project,' William says casually, as though being modest and gracious in the face of his bountiful generosity. 'As it happens, I know a lot about it. Anna's kept me well informed and I'm very interested in the subject. I think I could put the whole thing into its sociological context.'

Alison exchanges glances with Paula and tries to stifle a giggle.

'That might be a good idea, William,' Dana says without irony. 'We'll have to see. Well, I'm sorry to interrupt your work as usual. One of these days, Maggie Bushnell is going to have to ban me from this place. I'm sure I do this much too often.'

She applies some lipstick and ties a chiffon scarf around her neck. 'Now I look almost human. Bye, I'll be seeing you.'

She rushes out of the door, leaving Alison and Paula to look at each other in baffled concern.

32

Cruppled Sheets

DANA strips the bed in the spare room of Margot's flat where she has been staying and Hilary crawls out from underneath it.

'Hello, I didn't know you were there,' Dana laughs.

'*Peep-ho!*' Hilary screams, jumping up and down. 'I made you a surprise, didn't I, Dana.'

'You sure did.' She heaves a crumpled sheet and spreads it neatly over the bed.

'My Mummy always irons the sheets every day before she makes the bed so they're not cruppled like that.'

'Oh,' Dana replies in disbelief.

'But never mind. I won't tell her you're lazy.'

Hilary edges round the bed, pulling at one corner of the sheet.

'I'm *not* lazy, Hilary. I'm just very tired.' Dana believes in treating children as intellectual equals.

'Why are you tired?'

'I just am.'

'But why?'

'I've been very busy.'

'But you haven't done anything. You've just been fast asleep. I know, because I came in when you weren't looking and you were fast asleep, and you were snoring very loudly.'

'God, do I really snore?' Dana says in alarm.

'Yes. It was a very, very loud breathing noise.'

'Well, maybe I was just breathing very clearly.' She wonders fleetingly whether it has been her snoring that has affected her relationship with Mike. 'You see, I do a lot of things in the week, so at the weekend I'm exhausted, like your mouse when it's been running round the table for two minutes.'

Hilary's latest acquisition is a clockwork mouse, whose bouts of frenzied crawling have sent Margot and Dana into fits of adolescent hysteria.

'Dana, come into the garden. I want to play with you, Look, it's all lovely and sunny outside.'

Dana stands by the window with Hilary and sees Margot sunbathing below on a chaise-longue, a pink maternity smock gathered loosely around her to hide her distended stomach. To her left Tony is carrying slabs of concrete up the garden path.

'Mummy!' Hilary shouts down to her and Margot stands up and shouts something back at her daughter who is standing on tiptoe. Dana lifts her up and Hilary pushes open the window.

'What did you say?' Hilary shouts.

'I said, "Don't open the window," Margot shouts back, "because once it's open, we can't get it shut again.'

'Oh, so sorry, Margot,' Dana calls down. 'It's my fault. I had no idea.'

'I know you didn't, don't worry,' Margot calls back.

Dana rushes into the garden, where Margot has resumed her lethargic sunbathing.

'Gee, I'm sorry, Margot, what'll you do about the window?'

'We'll have to get a carpenter in to close it,' Margot laughs. 'It's ridiculous. If I hadn't shouted, she wouldn't have opened it. I think it's expanded.'

'Sure, that's life. The harder you try to be efficient, the more disorganised everything gets. My attitude is just to stop trying and to do whatever you fancy, but it doesn't seem to get anywhere.' Dana crouches on the grass and pulls a clover, plucking off one of its three leaves. 'I wish I could find a four-leaved clover. I've only ever found one once, when I was about nine.'

'Did you have some luck after that?'

'I can't remember... let me think... Oh yes, I won a prize at my Sunday school concert for singing a hymn.'

'Is that when the reaction set in?' Margot asks, laughing.

'My dear Margot, I was reacting against anything and everything from the age of dot. I guess I was one of those horrible infants that kicked and scratched every day, and I've never stopped. But now when I scream out, nobody listens. They're all too busy screaming out themselves.'

'You have a very odd view of people and life.'

'Odd. Well, maybe I'm honest, not only with other people, but with myself. I don't pretend that life's a bed of roses, but on the other hand, I don't pretend that it's miserable or ennobling. I just look at it and say, "What the hell, who gives a damn!"'

'I give a damn,' Margot says, 'and so do a lot of people. You know, I don't think you're rebelling against the establishment or against society and materialism. I think you're rebelling against yourself. You're fighting the best instinct within you.'

Dana stands up, her face pale with anger. 'Margot, I guess this is going to be the end of a beautiful friendship, if you're going to start lecturing me like my goddamned father and the local vicar. All this garbage about love. I just don't feel loving. I don't feel like hating either. Why can't we be moderate? Why do we have to be romantic? Just because you two happen to have a love-nest—'

'It's hardly a love nest! In any case, it's not just us two. Love exists. It's a force in life. You can't deny it. You can't try to subdue it or tame it into some watered-down intellectualism.'

Dana sits down on the grass again. 'Gee, I'm sorry, Margot. I shouldn't have lost my temper like that. I guess I'm still immature.'

'But you're not, Dana. You don't give yourself a chance. You've built up a false image of yourself. I guess I don't really know what I'm trying to say, but maybe you need to give yourself a break – and give yourself time, before making any definite decisions.'

Dana hesitates before replying but finally says, 'Maybe you're right.'

33

An Administrative Error

PAULA sits staring in horror at the note in front of her. An administrative error has been made and she is responsible. Yes, she is not normally careless, nor has it been entirely her fault. It has been one of those unfortunate mistakes, hovering between arbitrary circumstances and lack of foresight.

Miss Bushnell stormed in an hour ago and made a huge scene about it in front of everyone in the office. Moreover, what had most upset Paula was that everyone seems to have enjoyed the scene. Alison, June and William sat there behind their typewriters, turning pink in an effort not to laugh, and the moment the figure of the Head Archivist has retreated behind the door, there was a loud outburst of laughter. Paula is well aware that the matter was bound to strike them as amusing: their natural tendency to levity makes this inevitable, but nobody has shown the least concern for her predicament.

Paula doesn't considers that she is unusually sensitive and yet it seems at this moment that the façade of fun, gaiety and bonhomie is purely superficial. It frightens her that a group of people can work together daily over a certain period of time and form relationships which are outwardly effective yet inwardly empty. What has hurt her most is Alison's attitude.

'Forget about it,' Alison says dismissively, adding, 'Anyway, it gave us a good laugh. I've been bored stiff all week. For goodness sake, make a few errors. At least we can have a juicy bit of drama to entertain us.'

Paula is both irritated by Alison's tired overworking of this old joke and angry at the assumption that the error has been down to her. Yet she feels it is pointless to try to explain matters or to attempt to exonerate herself. Alison stares inanely out of the window and there is a strange, dreary silence apart from June's noisy munching of a ginger biscuit and William's self-absorbed chatter as he holds an involved conversation with a friend on the phone.

Paula takes a pocket mirror from her handbag and gazes stonily at her own reflection. Her eyes, small and grey with astute, black pupils, gaze coolly back at her. Her cheekbones gleam, high and white, the skin practically translucent.

I must snap out of this, she mutters to herself and returns to her work quietly and with concentration, until soon the feeling of emptiness disperses and is replaced by calm absorption. She now feels pleasantly self-sufficient – a state and condition at which she is continually aiming – usually without success.

It does not seem to matter to her that she and Douglas can no longer communicate, nor that Alison's friendship with her, though amusing, now seems insubstantial and nebulous. Nor does it matter that she is working with people who have formed a network constructed out of trivial dialogue with each other, as though they are deranged spiders spinning out useless, unnecessary lengths of thread.

Simply to be and to think seems a satisfactory mode of existence.

The sun shines down clearly onto the bibliography she is checking. As so often, the lower portion of the page has crumbled away. She gazes at the soft edges where the corner has disappeared. How odd it seems that this edge is not clean cut but a gradual paring away of the paper. She is suddenly confounded by her consciousness of the minuteness of things. It seems curious that each piece of paper comprises so many tiny particles, that her body is a vast conglomeration of molecules and that the dust, shimmering on the table, is made up of a mixture of minute substances.

It seems that there in no limit to each individual object or person, for if dust can merge, so can fragments and objects and human beings. Why then does she have this wish to be self-sufficient? Is it possible – or even desirable? Just as there is something to be gained from sharing experience and communication, is there also something to be gained from remaining silent and pondering within oneself? After a moment's reflection it occurs to her that the latter state is at most a mere substitute for the former; something to be endured rather than to be sought after. Yet perhaps it is her fate to endure it.

The phone rings. Alison answers it and then gives a slow smile. 'It's for you, Paula,' she says knowingly.

'Hello,' Paula says calmly.

'Hello, this is Roger.'

'Who?' Paula replies absently and then the name sinks in. 'Oh… Roger… Hello. How are you?' Is her tone too warm? she wonders.

'Fine. And you?'

'Oh, yes. Very well, thank you.'

There is a long, embarrassing silence.

'How nice to—'

'I rang to tell—'

They both stop and say simultaneously, 'Oh, sorry,' and laugh.

There is another long silence and then Roger says very loudly, 'I rang to tell you that I'm coming round to the searchroom this afternoon for some research and I wondered if you'd like to meet me for dinner afterwards.'

'Yes… How nice. Thank you,' Paula replies a little more coolly.

'OK, I'll see you outside the town hall at six. Cheerio.'

'Goodbye.' Paula puts down the phone with a puzzled expression on her face. It seems odd to her that the phone call should have come at the one moment when Roger was completely absent from her thoughts, especially because she has been thinking about him a good deal in recent weeks, and for some reason, instead of being pleased at the invitation, she is slightly disturbed.

It is as though she wants the challenge of solitude and self-sufficiency, and as though she dreads the pain of another unsuccessful liaison from which she will only be able to extricate herself with difficulty, and which might cause each of them to perform personality contortions, as has happened with Douglas.

It seems to Paula that human beings are too complex and wayward for her liking. And yet, like all other events, the phone call has come about naturally and by instinct she has responded to it affirmatively. There is no easy solution and no opposing it. She simply has to endure the mountainous network of feelings which might grow up between them.

'Cheer up,' Alison says. 'You look terrible today.'

'Thank you. Now I feel even worse.'

They both laugh and when Paula looks down again the spot of sunlight has shifted from the corner of the torn page and her uncomfortable mood of intense self-awareness has evaporated.

34

The Admission

PAULA walks down the wet pavements with Roger, coolly observing the damp leaves of the trees glistening olive-green and black in night light. Mud squelches beneath their shoes and every now and then Paula finds herself slithering on a slimy patch, grabbing Roger's arm to prevent herself from falling.

She feels peaceful and yet alert. The gnawing worry that has been growing within her for the past few weeks as to whether Roger likes her has been dispersed and her thoughts, instead of being turned inwards on her own emotions, are directed outwards conjunctly with those of Roger.

It seems like a development of their sexuality that instead of focusing their thoughts upon one another, these are co-mingled and turned outwards onto the scene before them. How strange that Roger could be seeing the same object that she is seeing and yet undoubtedly he reacts differently to it, and it is in this difference that the gulf between them lies and that the desire for complete union is waylaid.

Yes it does not seem to matter. A gap has been bridged and Paula feels content to accept the gulf that lies between them, which can never be bridged, in the knowledge that there is a solid channel of communication between them. They walk in silence though an arcade of shops, the rain falling on her hair which now hangs in rats' tails down the back of her raincoat.

It strikes Paula suddenly and incongruously as amusing that she can actually feel so ardently about someone who is nearly bald. She notices the strand of damp black hair hanging over Roger's domed forehead, giving him a falsely academic appearance – she considers it false because, despite his academic achievements she regards him as basically warm and humorous, and this was what has attracted her to him.

She watches Roger's face, glowing in the rain, and wonders whether the jocularity is a front that he has developed to counterbalance a very different disposition; yet she senses that it is not a façade but the natural development of his ironic attitude to things. She always considers matter coolly and with scrupulous honesty. It is this somewhat bleak outlook which invests her with an apparent coldness. Roger, on the other hand, is incapable of seeing anything as it is, for the moment he directs his gaze upon something, a mechanism in him transmutes it into comedy or to exaggeration. She is intrigued by this tendency to caricature reality, in contrast to her own tendency to downplay it.

A lorry rumbles past, and she wonders how they could have walked for such a long time in total silence. Yet it seems pointless to speak. Moreover she is convinced that anything that Roger might say would be a façade even beyond his normal façade, so when he suddenly stops in the doorway of a tobacconists and opens his mouth as if to speak, she sighs, anticipating what would seem like a mockery of her exalted mood. But instead his face appears strangely solemn and grey in the evening light.

'You've probably been wondering why I haven't tried to contact you before,' he says, 'since you now know how I feel about you. I mean, it's been a very long time since I last saw you and in a way, it was rather odd suddenly to ring you up out of the blue like I did.'

Paula nods in silent assent, thinking how simple his words sound for a change.

'I wanted to get in touch with you before,' he says, 'but I couldn't.' He looks empty and incongruously angry.

Paula knows that she ought to ask why, but simply feels too lethargic to move. There is a long silence.

'Why not?' she asks dully, anticipating some unpleasant piece of information.

'Because,' he says and smiles.

'Oh, I see,' Paula laughs bleakly.

'Because I'm bloody well married.' He smirks stupidly.

Paula stares at him in amazement. She has been expecting something unpleasant, such as pressure of work or some other involvement. For one moment she suspected a homosexual liaison, because of his pointed embarrassment, but the thought of a wife has, for some reason, never entered her mind. She suddenly realises why he looks so angry. It is he who has had to take the initiative and he is in an impossible situation.

'Not only that,' he adds. 'Our marriage went off the rails about five years ago.'

Paula makes a mental note that he must be in his early forties and realises she doesn't usually fall in love with men who are considerably older than herself.

'I see,' she says flatly.

'But that's not the point. You don't see. That's not the point at all. If it were just that I could get a divorce…'

He almost seems to be directing his anger towards Paula. She stares open-mouthed.

'But I can't, and that's the point.'

Her thoughts are caught up between curiosity as to why he can't and a reflection that he has repeated the same phrases at least three times. She also feels a terrible emptiness, realising that her former elation has been utterly unfounded.

'Why not? Why ever not? For goodness sake, get it out.' Paula is trembling with agitation.

'Well, my wife… she's contracted multiple sclerosis and I'm looking after her. That's why not.' His voice is flat and empty.

'But you said that your marriage had failed long ago. Couldn't she go into a home or something?'

Looking up at him, Paula realises that this must sound utterly absurd as they have known each other so briefly. Even so, he smiles at her and draws her closely to him.

'You know how I feel about you, Paula,' he says softly. 'But I just can't do it. I mean, the marriage failed as far as I was concerned, and we separated – I moved out – but… well, she still clung to me and she besieged me with letters and phone calls after I'd left her and then, when she got ill, I felt I had to look after her and…'

'I know. It's stupid of me when there are obviously so many factors I didn't know about. I'm sure it must be hard for both of you and you're doing the best thing. Oh God, I'm so bloody selfish, I feel so terrible. It's stupid of me and the whole thing was all in my mind anyway.'

'But it wasn't,' he insists, kissing her, 'and you must know that after tonight.'

He presses her into a shop doorway and she starts to cry, not because of what he has just told her, but out of happiness that he does in fact love her. She isn't used to crying and only cries out of joy. As the rain falls down in sheets onto the pavements, and Paula stands in the doorway trembling and crying, with Roger looking empty and angry beside her, she feels how absurd everything is and it seems as though they have exchanged personalities, for a flicker of mockery appears at the corner of her mouth, while Roger's face is devoid of expression as he gazes with open eyes at the falling rain.

35

Total Consciousness

WILLIAM sits on the park bench, holding up a small square mirror in his hands.

'You shouldn't keep looking at yourself in the mirror, William,' Anna says, taking a book out of her shoulder-bag. 'It seems really vain and narcissistic – and actually quite effeminate.'

'I'm not admiring myself. I'm trying to really see myself.'

'What do you mean?'

'Well, I'm trying to see the real me beyond the confines of my social identity. Can I exist in a vacuum? Can there be a "me" without anybody there to see me? Do I actually exist?'

He is peering at a spot on his chin closely in the mirror.

Anna laughs. 'I think games like that are very dangerous.'

'Of course you do. You're afraid to explore yourself, because your one attempt to do so was totally unsuccessful and you had a breakdown.'

Anna opens the book, a Penguin edition of *Madame Bovary*, and placing the bookmark in the pocket of her handbag, she yawns. 'I'm so tired of all that. Why can't you just live?'

'I want to be totally aware. There's a general assumption that it's impossible to be totally conscious of every emotion, every thought and feeling all at the same time, so we deliberately block out most of our consciousness. I want to challenge this acceptance of living with only a minimum of awareness. I am aiming for total consciousness, even if it's pure hell.'

Anna sighs. 'You're already well on the way to the bin yourself if you're thinking along those lines.'

'But Anna, I'm not being irrational. I want to catch a glimpse of reality. For instance, I'll give you an example. In your feelings towards any one person, there are a whole host of conflicting elements. Maybe you think you like that person, but there's a streak of jealousy, or maybe you think you hate them, but there's a streak of desire for them. All the time and every day we deliberately deceive ourselves. Well, I hate this deceit. I want to know what I really feel.'

'You speak as though that's the true reality, William, but it's not. We cannot expect to somehow miraculously gain insight, understanding and wisdom of all knowledge in one lifetime, let alone in a few minutes. And sometimes too much truth and honesty when you're not prepared for it can be very destructive. I should know…'

'Why not,' William says, ignoring the implications of what she had just said and thumping his skinny knee. 'Because we're brought up to think in a very narrow way. We're hoodwinked into conforming to certain social stereotypes of what is considered "normal living" – we allow ourselves to be organised in restrictive patterns and we're brainwashed into having fixed attitudes. But underneath we are a kaleidoscope, a myriad of impressions and perceptions and sensations and ideas. That's the whole excitement of life – these conflicts and incongruities – and I want to capture it.'

Anna sighs again.

'For instance,' William continues undaunted, 'suppose you go into a restaurant to have a meal by yourself – why *do* you? Because you're hungry. And why by yourself? Because there happens to be no-one around to eat with. And when you do sit down to eat, you say to yourself, "Although I've come in of my own free will, I don't really want to eat by my-self here."'

'But at the same time, you're hiding from yourself the fact that there's an element of excitement in eating by yourself, because it's contrary to your inclinations and programming, and maybe subconsciously you want people to look at you and say, "Who is that person and why are they eating all by themselves?"'

'Oh William,' Anna laughs, 'you are funny. In fact, you're quite a scream.'

It's William's turn to sigh. 'Scream is the right word. Sometimes I think my novel is a scream, a wail, a howl, rather than a mass of words.'

'Have you put all these ideas into your novel?'

'Yes, only I've embedded them within events and actions, so that they can only be recognised by perceptive readers.'

'And what about unperceptive ones?'

'Too bad. They can go to hell. I don't want idiots reading my book.'

'But maybe they're just the people who ought to be read-ing your book. All those other perceptive ones have probably had the same thoughts as you years ago.'

William's face sags visibly. 'That's true,' he says, looking almost crestfallen.

'Don't worry, I'm only teasing,' she smiles.

William peers again at his reflection in the mirror. 'One eye is green and the other is blue-grey,' he says anxiously. 'Do you think that's significant of anything?'

'Yes, you're a freak.'

'It's significant to me, because I always have two points of view about everything.'

'Oh William, can't you give it a rest for today?'

'Well, I'm trying to be as creative as possible. I make a deliberate attempt to be creative all the time and I reckon maybe ten per cent of it is genuine creativity. The rest is just fantasy and bullshit.'

'I wish I could develop my imagination like that. I suppose it might come with years of practice, but some people are born gifted. I wish I was.'

'Don't we all,' William says as the wind blows Anna's hair horizontally at right angles to her head.

'My God, you look like a tortured statue – Boadicea or one of the Greek Furies – with your hair flying behind you.'

Anna doesn't seem to hear him but gets up from the bench. 'I'm going back to the hostel now, William.'

'I'm sorry, I've been talk a load of rubbish today.'

'Just for a change,' she laughs.

'Well, I suppose it's back to the rat-race. I can't wait to start stuffing envelopes again. It's such fun – and so mind-expanding. Whoopee.'

36

Nuisance Calls

ALISON sits lethargically staring into space. She takes a delight in doing as little work as possible, not regarding this as laziness, but rather as an economic expenditure of energy. Since, however, she applies this principle all the time, the object tends to defeat its purpose because she never puts much vigour into anything and consequently has a superfluous store of energy. She is feeling serene at this moment, or perhaps this serenity is merely an absence of thought or conflict. Whatever the mood is, she savours it, breathing deeply by the half-open window and gazing at the pale-blue sky, broken at intervals by chimneys and trees.

The phone rings and she answers it. 'Good morning, Bridchester Records Office.'

'Hello, Alison, I recognised your voice.'

'Oh, hello, Aunty Fiona – how are you?'

'Very well, thank you – and how are you?'

The conversation continues in this stilted fashion for around ten minutes, during which both sides are guarded, hesitating to give out any details of their private lives or to express any genuine emotion, and consequently the contact, though verbal, is essentially non-existent.

'Well, I'll see you next week then. Goodbye,' Fiona concludes briskly.

'Goodbye,' Alison says half-heartedly, putting the phone down and resuming the lethargic contemplation of her typewriter.

'God, families,' she says to William.

'I know, they're pernicious, aren't they. Always forcing themselves on you. I just long to get away from mine and they will keep insisting that I ring them up or go home to see them. It's such a bloody nuisance.'

'Actually that's not my problem. I wouldn't mind if my family were genuinely warm. I say "my family", but in fact it only consists of my uncle and aunt. The trouble is I've never had much of a relationship with either of them – but although they have no interest in me as a person, they can be very demanding. We have to keep up this continual pretence and it really gets on my wick.'

'You were an only child, weren't you?' William asks solicitously.

Paula looks surprised at this sudden contact between William and Alison, who are usually at loggerheads.

'Yes,' Alison replies, 'and in fact I didn't even get on with my mother. I never saw my father. He was away in the air force most of the time and my mother got depressed and bored and resentful and took it all out on me.'

'Well, perhaps it made you a stronger character,' June suggests, though she feels a little embarrassed by Alison's candour.

'No it didn't. It just means that I can't really love anybody.'

Paula, emerging from the cupboard at the other end of the room, looks up in surprise and then hides her face again in the cupboard, as embarrassed as June.

'You see, Steve loves me more than I love him.'

'Perhaps things will change,' William says.

Alison ignores the remark. 'My mother uses to criticise me whatever I did. For instance, one day I bought a sweater – I was only fourteen and I wanted to look trendy. And then I went to stay with a friend for a few days and when I got back she'd thrown it away... well, she hadn't literally thrown it in the dustbin, but she'd given it to our cleaning lady, without even consulting me – of all the cheek.'

She pauses, leaning forward and hugging her arms together, as if bracing herself to recall the past.

'And she used to do that sort of thing the whole time. It just got me down and in the end we were hardly on speaking terms. At one point we were even passing messages to each other through my aunt.'

She laughs and it is clear to Paula that Alison still harbours a deep, unconscious affection for her mother, in that she seems to exist in her mind as a living person even after he death.

'And the way she used to cook meals. It was absolutely frightful. I'm sure she'd have kittens if she could see some of the recipes I make these days. She always did meat and two veg, and the vegetables were always boiled for too long so they were practically tasteless. It's not surprising that I have this craving for exotic food —'

'At least you don't eat chocolate-covered locust,' William says. 'A friend of mine was telling me last night that he ate a whole plate of them before he knew what they were and as soon as he found out he was violently sick.'

'Well, I wouldn't got that far in my taste for original dishes,' Alison says. 'Actually, I like to do really unusual things with very ordinary ingredients. That's half the fun, to create something wonderful out of something dull and boring.'

'It's like my writing really,' William says. 'I like to take the mundane substance of life and transmute it into the extraordinary and—'

'OK,' Paula sighs, 'what about some work this morning? Bushnell's popping in at some point to inspect the shelves and I gather she thinks we've talking rather too much recently.'

'I wonder where she got that idea from?' Alison says.

'I think human intercourse is more important than—'

'But we're not paid to chat, William. We're paid to work,' Paula points out, and then concedes, 'I agree with you, but you know…'

'We do indeed,' Alison agrees with a smile and begins to type vigorously.

37

Chinese Patterns

PAULA sits in amazement in her bedroom, wondering what to do. Her landlady has decided to sell all her properties and as a result she has a month's notice to leave. It is not so much the move that upsets Paula but rather the unpredictability of it all.

Mrs Anderson has always seemed so dependable – a figure in the background on whom she could rely – and the sudden decision causes her to perceive the difficulty of drawing any conclusions about people. If a slight acquaintance could be so fickle, could a close friend or even a lover be likewise? She reflects upon Roger's honesty and frankness. If she were ever to find any duplicity in his behaviour, she would be desolate. Yet it is a possibility she has to consider.

If this were the case and no one was utterly reliable, could she then develop the necessary self-reliance to protect herself in future? She stares at the Chinese patterns on the carpet and gazing into a red pentangle, she realises that the aim of her inner life is to achieve what she terms to herself 'spiritual creativity'.

She is conscious of the twin desires to improve herself morally and intellectually. It sounds so glib, yet it is so difficult to achieve and once begun it has to be sustained. The continuous effort is what frightens Paula. She is aware of an apathy in herself, which confounds such aims, yet she is determined to overcome this.

Moreover, her natural tendency to be optimistic is often undermined by her sensitivity. For instance, her reciprocated love for Roger should be a source of joy, yet it is not. Instead she feels a continual pain that they cannot achieve an open relationship and also the anxiety that he might cease to love her.

It seems to her that she is perhaps deliberately creating unhappy situations, although her actual life situation is comparatively simple. She reflects on William, who on the contrary has so many problems and yet somehow manages to remain totally irrepressible. This morning he walked into the office, his hands swathed in bandages...

*

'Have you hurt yourself?' Alison asked.

'Well, it doesn't actually hurt, but it looks pretty weird.'

He swiftly undid the dressing to reveal an enormous green lump on his hand. They all averted their eyes in revulsion.

'Pretty gruesome, isn't it. I did it making coffee last night. I was so sleepy that I stuck my hand in front of the kettle. I gave a huge scream and the bloke next door came rushing in. He said I looked a right twit, standing there screaming with a scalded hand.'

'Shouldn't you have it seen to?' asked Paula anxiously.

'No, it's all right, so long as it's covered up, and I mustn't pierce it, whatever I do. I shudder to think what's formed inside that lump.'

Alison looked again, in spite of herself, and retched slightly before looking away.

'Mind you, I've always been a good patient,' William went on.

'William, you're marvellous and we all know it,' Alison said. 'Now shut up about your bloody lump, for goodness sake.'

*

Paula smiles as she recalls the scene. If the same thing had happened to her, she would probably have created a tragedy out of it, which she would of course have then downplayed. She fishes an evening paper out of her shopping-basket. As usual her reflections are totally irrelevant to her situation. She scans the 'Flats to Let' column and tries to decide whether a large flat on the outskirts of Bridchester would be better than a tiny one in the centre, or whether an attic in a converted church hall would be more desirable than either.

Another problem she has to face is how to finish with Douglas when he returns next week. She switches on the radio and starts listening to a play, but within a few minutes she has fallen asleep in her armchair with her newspaper tucked underneath one elbow and her skirt caught up on one of the arms of the chair. Awoken by the ringing of the doorbell, she staggers to the door and opens it.

Roger walks in, smiling and slightly pink, like a cheerful gnome with a mischievous air, as though about to confide in her about some secret misdeed, but instead sits down on the chair opposite and gazes at her mildly. Paula gazes back smiling, her eyes travelling over his domed forehead, dark eyes and then chin. In repose his expression is penetrating and intelligent.

'You look dreadful,' he says. 'What's up?'

'Oh, just about everything,' Paula says. 'I'm feeling pretty cheesed off. My landlady's given me notice to quit. I don't mind going actually, but it's thrown me. It takes me a little time to adapt to new situations. I suppose I want everything to be permanent.'

'Don't we all, but it's about time you grew up.'

'Oh don't start lecturing me. Well anyway, there's nothing decent to let in the papers. I'll probably end up in some crumby hostel for spinster schoolteachers.'

'That would suit you,' Roger laughs.

'So what should I do?'

'I don't know, we could always get a flat together, if—'

'Don't talk rubbish... How's *Molly* today?' she adds pointedly.

'Mmm... a bit better, actually. But as you're moving, you could get a flat closer to me. It'll save me this inconvenient journey.'

'Roger, I'm just too tired and stressed for your facetious jokes.'

'Sorry. You do sound very, very tired.' He flops on the floor beside her and puts his head in her lap. 'So am I, to tell the truth. Tired and fed up with all this. This situation is hell, Utter hell. It's really getting me down.'

'Don't, Roger. There's no need to be. We ought to be happy.'

'But we're not, because we want more of each other than just a few days here and there. I know it's a cliché but the more I see you, the more I want to see you.'

'It all sounds romantic, but we're really being very stupid. I mean clandestine affairs are pretty much the same all
over the world.'

'Don't call this a clandestine affair, Paula – don't make a
mockery of what we've got.'

'I'm *not* trying to make a mockery of it. I'm just trying to
be rational. I mean, I feel just as bad as you do.'

'Well, what can we bloody do?'

'Nothing, except go on existing from day to day and try
to find some satisfaction in the situation as it is. We just have
to face reality.'

'I know, I know, but I can't say it's OK,' he sighs, pulling
her onto the rug beside him.

38

Plausibility and Impact

DANA is in a bad temper by the time she arrives at the writers' club. As usual in Bridchester during the past few weeks, it has been pouring with rain and her green dress is clinging damply to her body beneath her coat. She walks in hastily and makes for the electric heater, fanning her hands in front of the heat to get dry. After a few minutes she begins to thaw out and relaxes.

As usual each club member has to read out a short piece of work, which is followed by criticism from the other members. Dana reads aloud a short story she scribbled hastily yesterday morning on the bus and then typed out late last night. It describes her very first meeting with Mike and emphasises what she now regards as his phoneyness, his posturing and posing.

There is a chorus of feedback, commenting on defects in style and technical errors – and as if to complement the subject matter of her story, she detects a falseness in the writers' circle itself. Yet nobody has commented on the actual content of the story. Just as this thought occurs to her, a tall man gets up from a corner of the room and moves over to stand beside her. He snatches the typewritten sheets and scans them hastily. Dana stares at him in amazement.

'Where is that sentence,' he asks in an eastern European accent, 'the one about Gordon being empty and phoney?'

Dana finds the sentence, which takes up a whole paragraph at the bottom of the second page. He reads it and declares with satisfaction, 'This is a comment on you yourself, I think.'

Dana looks up in bewilderment. The personal remark is totally out of keeping with the character and ethos of the club, and although she is not bound by conventions, she sets great store by good manners. She winces at his familiarity and plain rudeness. Other members clearly feel the same and a chorus of protest follows.

'Oh Jan!'

'Shut up!'

'That's not fair!'

'Dana, don't listen to Jan,' Madeleine says. 'He talks a lot of rubbish and we always ignore him.'

But Dana suddenly find herself reacting to this mass hostility to Jan. 'No, he's right,' she says. 'It could be true.'

Jan carries on reading page two. 'And this. What does this mean: "lyrical vitality"?'

'It doesn't mean anything,' she says quietly.

There is a subdued silence and Dana realises that everyone is staring at her, waiting expectantly for her to do or say something. In defiance of this, she continues to sit there, saying nothing.

'Why all this pretence? It's not your real self,' Jan persists.

Dana immediately reacts again, feeling hostile and embarrassed. 'It's only a story and I'm not a goddamned professional, for God's sake. I just write for fun.'

'Come on, Jan,' Madeleine intervenes. 'Let's hear the latest chapter of your saga. Then we can all pull *you* to pieces.' She rubs her hands together in gleeful anticipation.

Jan proceeds to read at great length and haltingly a long chapter describing his father's exploits in the war. Dana gathers from the narrative that he is Polish. The English is simple and the narrative style is characterised by brief sentences and a great deal of repetitious dialogue. Surprisingly, the ensuing criticism is mild from everyone except William, who lets forth a torrent of critical suggestions.

'It shouldn't be written in the first person,' he says. 'It should be in the third person, and you must prune down the style. There's too much verbiage and—'

'I disagree,' Dana interrupts.

'Let's hear your views, Dana,' Madeleine says.

'I don't think it should be in the third person at all. The best thing about it is its plausibility and impact, and this comes directly from being in the first person. It wouldn't be nearly so effective in the third person.'

She pauses, waiting for Jan to react, but he simply sits there, gazing at her intensely.

'At the moment,' she concludes awkwardly, 'it's like a slice of life and you've got to—'

'Time for tea,' Madeleine announces loudly, pointing to a trolley laden with tea and cakes.

The meeting breaks up into informal chatter once again and Dana and Jan are left sitting staring at each other in silence: total strangers who have made a peculiar kind of contact, highly personal in one sense but purely literary in another.

Dana suddenly feels tired and unwilling to be sociable. She remains seated, her dress still clinging damply round her knees, yawning at intervals, while Jan wanders back to his corner to tall to someone else. Dana, meanwhile, picks up a book of Japanese poems from Madeleine's bookshelf and, oblivious to the noise around her, stretches our her legs in front of the fire and begins to read them, whispering aloud odd couplets to herself.

She is so absorbed in the poems that she doesn't notice Jan, as he sits down clumsily beside her again.

'What are you reading?'

Dana cannot be bothered to reply but instead hands him the book, simultaneously yawning. She is ashamed of her momentary attraction towards him, which has caused her to defend his work so vociferously, and now she surveys him coolly. He is in his late thirties and she senses that his aggressiveness is a front, a cover-up for shyness. Yet she does not feel disposed to penetrate this barrier. She herself, though often antisocial, has never been shy, and tends to feel a mixture of protectiveness and pity for those who are.

Jan sits there awkwardly, and she notices the oiliness of his black hair and wonders whether he uses some kind of hair oil. It seems oddly old-fashioned and outdated. His face is taut with the effort to make sense of the couplets and he shifts uncomfortably on his chair as Dana scrutinises his face. Eventually she laughs.

'I don't know why we all try and be intellectual here,' she says, glancing casually round the room.

Jan looks up and takes in the room and the deafening conversation around him.

'Don't try to be so clever,' he says.

'I'm not – they are.'

'They're not – you are.'

Dana grins amicably and he gazes at her with frank enjoyment. She looks at him with weary cynicism and after an enormous effort of will, she stands up, says goodbye to the assembled group and hastily departs, leaving Jan smiling to himself.

39

Shin Cracks

A FEW days later as Dana comes out of the cinema, her eyes readjusting to the white afternoon light, she is hovering outside the foyer, studying the stills from the film, when a hand claps itself on top of the photograph within the central area of her vision. She looks around in annoyance to find Jan, in a creased white raincoat and carrying a child's satchel, looking down at her in amusement, smiling at her surprise.

'What a lousy movie,' Dana says.

'I enjoyed it very much. I particularly liked the simple background music, violin and accordion. It really gave one the atmosphere of the 1930s.'

'I'd rather do without all that. Anyway all that cute French retro folk is pretty dated, isn't it?'

'You put everything into compartments. It's too reductive and simplistic.'

Dana is not in the mood for subtleties. 'God, I'm late. I've got to call on the Electricity Board for a friend of mine.'

'Which way is that?'

'Down Queen Street – near the Indian restaurant.'

'Oh yes, I love the smell of curry that floats all the way down the street,' Jan says, accompanying her as she turns left.

Dana finds it irritating that not only is he banal but apparently persistent.

'Tell me,' he says casually, 'are you doing anything tonight?'

'Yes,' she replies stonily. 'I'm babysitting for my friend.'

'Why?'

'Because she's going out.'

'Why do you stay in? Why don't you go out and enjoy yourself.'

Dana groaned. 'Look, I don't feel like having discussions about what I do and don't like to do.'

'So you *do* like to stay in,' he persists.

'Yes.' She raises her voice slightly. 'I'm doing it to help out my friend. I happen to be sensitive to other people's feelings, which you obviously aren't.'

By now they have reached the Electricity Board office and showroom.

'Why am I not?'

'Because you keep questioning me the whole time,' she snaps.

'Don't you like being asked questions?'

Dana, despite her determination to rebuff him and remain cold and aloof, cannot help laughing. 'No, it's such a bore.'

'I'm surprised. I thought—'

'OK, OK, Look, I'm pretty busy. Now I must go in and talk to this man, so I'll say goodbye.'

Jan takes a pad out of his pocket and writing something on it, hands the scrap of paper to Dana. 'Just give me a ring if you feel like it,' he says casually.

'Sure, sure. As I said before, I'm pretty busy these days.'

'Oh, life is one mad rush,' he mocks in a Polish version of an upper-class English accent.

'Yeah, you could put it that way,' she smiles. 'So long.'

She turns into the showroom and does not look round. When she emerges ten minutes later, it is raining, She runs quickly down the street and skids and falls to the ground on a patch of slimy leaves clustered around the base of a tree. Still half in thought, she shudders as her shin cracks against the pavement and feels a sharp pain. For a moment she is incapable of thought, the pain is so intense. She lies half-straddled on the ground, shivering as two men pass by and gesticulate, as if to help her up.

'No,' she gasps. 'Please leave me alone. I'll be OK in a minute.'

She motions for them to go away and they retreat, looking back anxiously in her direction. Dana takes several deep breaths, trying to control the pain. As each throb seizes her, she attempts to reason with herself that pain can be beneficial – a learning experience. But as each wave passes, she turns alternately hot and cold, and feels the pain gaining control over her thoughts so that her mind is void, reflecting only acute agony.

For several minutes her vision blackens, she sees stars in front of her eyes and feels dizzy and thirsty; then, making an enormous effort, she opens her eyes very wide and in the distance sees Jan walking back down the road in her direction. He is looking in the shop windows as he walks.

'Oh God, no,' she mutters and dragging herself up, she staggers into a nearby café. As she heaves herself into a seat by the window, she sees him walking past, slowly and thoughtfully. She scrutinises his face, which is fortunately averted from her. It is pale and sad, the thin corners of the mouth drooping slightly and the cheekbones jutting out.

Dana orders coffee and wonders to herself why she takes such delight in rejecting him. Is it simply because she doesn't want to become involved again so soon after Mike, or is she perhaps being sadistic? It is obvious that she and Jan communicate well, even though most of their conversation so far has been like a sparring match.

She can tell that he is seeking something, whether misguidedly or not, beyond the daily routine of living. She can envisage their friendship being at first intense and then fading out, leaving them both disappointed. Yet is this a fair conjecture? Perhaps it would be better not to engage in hypothetical projections, but simply accept what appears to be his genuine interest in her and see what happens.

As she sips her coffee and her body begins to relax after the fall, she tries to analyse her attitude towards pain. It is far removed from a religious belief that suffering is ennobling, and yet she feels that it certainly causes her to think more deeply about things, if only in stark contrast to the moments of agony, when thought is no longer possible.

Dana realises that although people often term her 'thoughtless', it is alien to her nature to inflict pain. She recalls again Jan's drooping face as he walked past the window, and taking the scrap of paper he gave her, she makes a decision.

40

Flat-Leaving Parties

'PAULA'S late this morning,' Alison says. 'Probably clearing up the mess after the party.'

'I don't know what her landlady will say about the state we left the flat in,' William says.

'Flat-leaving parties always end up by trashing them. Steve said he saw some bloke stubbing out fag ends on the carpet, and he was sure he saw some scorched holes when he checked it later. Some people go completely crazy at parties. What time did you get home, June?'

'Oh, around four this morning. Mind you, there were still people staggering between the kitchen and bathroom when we left at 3.30. I think she provided too much food. And that pâté was very rich.'

'Well, you can't please everybody,' Alison says. 'And what did you think of Roger, her new bloke?'

'I was going to ask you about him,' June says. 'I'm sure I've seen him around before. Is he a lecturer at—'

'Yes, and he's married to boot.'

'Oh Lord – that's not like our Paula to steal other women's husbands.'

'I gather she didn't exactly steal him. It just sort of happened,' Alison says, bundling a parcel into the cupboard. 'And for goodness sake, don't tease her about him. She's very sensitive about the whole thing – and she seems to be crazy about him.'

'Really – and what about the wife?'

'She's an invalid, I gather, and he—'

'Ssshhh,' June warns. 'Here she comes.'

They hear Paula coming up the stairs and she enters the office looking tired and disconsolate. 'Well, I'm glad you all made it on time. I was up until six throwing people out.'

'They were enjoying themselves,' June laughs. 'Thanks for inviting us. Tom and I had a lovely time.'

'Good. I'm glad someone did,' Paula says curtly, hanging her coat up. Her face is pale and strained.

'But Paula, it was terrific, really it was,' Alison says. 'Steve and I enjoyed it no end.'

'Oh I couldn't give a damn if the bloody party was a success,' Paula snaps. 'Roger bloody well came after I told him not to and now there'll be rumours going round Bridchester and as soon as his wife hears about us... God, I—'

'But you can't expect him not to come when you've been seeing such a lot of each other. So you didn't invite him?'

'Not only did I *not* invite him but I gave him specific orders *not* to come. It was a direct non-invitation.'

'That's an interesting concept – a variation on "disinvitation",' William begins. 'I believe it was Engels who said—'

'Shut up, William,' Alison shouts, going up to Paula's chair and resting her hand firmly on the back of it. 'Look, you've got to face things, Paula. You can't have your cake and eat it, you know. Either you do go out with the bloke or you don't and... oh, goodness, please don't cry.'

Paula has not in fact burst into tears, but instead is pressing two fingers between her eyes.

'I think I've got a headache coming on,' she says. 'Sorry, I'll get over this.' She turns round to everybody and flashes a careless smile. 'I'm glad you all enjoyed it. It's funny – I've been at that flat for over a year and that's the first party I've given. I have no idea what Mrs Anderson will say when she sees the state of the carpet.'

William runs his fingers through his hair and Paula observes with distaste the long fingernails grey with dirt.

'People do tend to behave differently in crowds. It's the herd mentality. You can see examples of it in football hooliganism and then of course there was Nazi Germany—'

'I hope you're not comparing my party to a Wembley cup final, let alone a Nuremberg Rally, William. Speaking of people acting differently, though, I noticed how changed Anna was. She's quite lively now.'

William looks rather subdued at this remark and nods pensively.

'I noticed her going home with that odd bloke – the one that Dana came with,' June says. 'He and Dana were having a terrific row on the stairs. Did you notice?'

'No,' Paula says in surprise. 'When was that?'

'Oh, about ten minutes after they arrived – and they came quite early. But I did think Dana was being very unpleasant to him.'

'Really?' Alison says. 'What did she say?'

'Well, I don't remember all of it – and most of it is unrepeatable – but it was mainly to the effect that she wished she hadn't brought him. I think he made some kind of political comment, which annoyed her, because she kept calling him a right-wing bigot and a hypocrite and—'

'That's odd,' Paula says, 'because I don't remember seeing Dana at all at the party.'

'No?' June says. 'Well, she left after the Big Row. He
didn't seem to mind particularly. He got quite pally with
Anna. I noticed them huddled up together and—'

'Oh, stop gossiping,' William snaps. 'It gets on my
nerves.'

They all look up in surprise and see him fidgeting with
his staple-remover, his face contorted in a concentrated effort
to make the gadget work.

Paula glances meaningfully at Alison, who smiles slowly
and they turn the conversation to the rising rate of research
students at the university.

41

Alison's Aunt

ALISON studies herself in the fitting-room mirror. The red dress looks magnificent beneath the fluorescent lighting, the high collar emphasising her cheekbones, which stand out beneath her translucent skin. Tossing back her head, she smooths down her hair and flicks it into a neat bunch behind her ears.

The dress makes her look elegant – even alluring: every movement of her tall, slim body is exaggerated by the cut of the dress, with its long sleeves and large commerbund. It is a pity, she thinks, that she did not have it in time for Paula's party.

As she exits the fitting room she sees the face of the shop assistant looking admiringly at her.

'Ooh, that's lovely. Are you going to take it?'

'Yes,' Alison replies, changing back into her trouser suit.

An hour later she is walking up the steps to her aunt's mansion flat, situated in a block of villas on the outskirts of Bridchester. Alison is in the habit of dropping in every few weeks for tea, in an effort to maintain the reputation that her family, though small, is close-knit, in spite of what she has admitted to Paula and co. at the records office about the true nature of their relationship.

Her uncle is still at work and Fiona is in the middle of watching a swimming gala on television.

'Come in. I'm just watching the Nice finals. Can you see all right there?'

'Yes, fine, thank you.'

For the next hour neither of them say a word as they gaze at the black and white screen. Eventually the clock in the hall strikes five and Fiona bustles out to make tea, which she serves ten minutes later, again in silence.

'How's Uncle George?' Alison asks, forcing herself to make conversation.

'Not too good, I'm afraid. Oh dear, look at that man. He's shivering to death.' She passes Alison a plate of biscuits. 'His knee's been playing up again. I keep telling him to go and see an osteopath, but you know your uncle – he's so obstinate.'

She turns back to the television again and leaning back in her chair, crosses her legs and folds her arms, an expression of intelligent concentration on her face, as though solving some advanced complex mathematical problem relating to quantum physics.

'I suppose I ought to be getting back soon,' Alison says.

'Really dear?' her aunt replies absently.

Alison suddenly has an idea. 'Would you like to see my dress?'

'Mmm.'

She goes into Fiona's bedroom, changes into the dress and combs back her hair. The effect is even more flattering than in the shop. Delighted that she has at last found some common ground over which she can communicate with her aunt, she walks back expectantly into the living room and stands to one side of the television set.

'Oh dear, it's much too short.'

'What do you mean? It's the same length as my skirt.'

'No, it's *much* shorter.'

'But nobody worries about length these days. I mean, at the office, everybody comes in with different length dresses. It simply doesn't matter, as long as it looks nice.'

'It's a pity you should be the one to be wearing the wrong length,' her aunt replies, shaking her head lugubriously. 'And what's that thing above the waist. Is it a shadow or a piece of dust?'

Alison looks down and rubs her fingers over the area, but the mark stubbornly remains.

'It's soiled,' Fiona declares triumphantly. 'I bet they were jolly pleased to get rid of a dress like that – too short and soiled. They've pulled a fast one on you.'

'But I chose it myself.'

'It doesn't matter. I expect they were delighted. They saw *you* coming, and no mistake! You really should be more careful.'

'But it doesn't matter. I can easily wash it off.'

'That won't wash off. It'll have to be cleaned. What a waste of good money to—'

'Oh, don't make such a fuss,' Alison shouts, on the verge of losing her temper. 'A tiny little mark… It's a gorgeous dress. Don't keep on about it.'

'But you should be more careful.'

'Well, you know the sort of person I am. I'll never change. I don't notice things like that. All my life I'll go on choosing pretty dresses which may be slightly marked and I promise you, I won't give a damn!'

Fiona turns back to the television, still shaking her head knowingly.

'Aunty Fiona!' Alison shouts. 'Look at me. Don't just sit there watching the telly the whole time. I'm trying to tell you something.'

Fiona gazes up at her pityingly. 'I know. You've told me. If you're the sort of person who can't even buy clothes sensibly by yourself, then you should go with somebody.'

'For God's sake, I'm twenty-four. It's only a tiny little mark and if you think—'

At this point her uncle enters the room and looks at them both in amazement. They rarely quarrel, mainly because their contact is usually confined to brief pleasantries.

'Uncle George, don't you think this dress suits me?'

'It's much too short and it's dreadfully soiled,' Fiona persists. 'But she won't listen to me. She'll just go her own way.'

'But I'm trying to communicate with you,' Alison shouts, 'and you won't communicate. You just sit there, all shut in and switched off.'

'What you'd like me to do is to agree with you. That's what you call communication – agreeing with you. You don't like it when I tell you the truth.'

Alison suddenly laughs at the truth of her aunt's words and then, like a sulky child, turns back to her uncle.

'Well, she didn't need to go on about it,' she says crossly.

42

Birthday Drinks

ALISON and Paula walk into the Plough with William and June in tow. William has offered to stand them all a drink, as it is his birthday. While he is ordering the drinks, June says wryly, 'Dare we ask how old the lad is?'

Alison grins. 'Judging by his behaviour, fifteen, but according to the laws of deduction, at least twenty-one, I'd say. In fact, probably older. He's done a bit of travelling, between school and university.'

'William's OK,' Paula says. 'He's not so bad. He was really concerned last night when someone fainted outside the town hall.'

'My God, yes. He talked about it non-stop for twenty minutes this morning, while you were in the searchroom. But I suppose I agree with you. I think he's basically just a human being trying to be a non-human. And when he washes, he can even look quite normal.'

'Normal's going a bit far – and I'm sure he would object to being called normal. His hair's quite a nice colour actually. What would you call it – blond or—'

'Biscuit, I'd call it,' June says. 'Digestive biscuit when it's washed; porridge with treacle when it isn't. If only he wouldn't buy all his clothes from jumble sales, he'd be quite smart.'

'His new fur coat's got a bald patch, just below the collar. Did you notice?' Alison says, and then feels a pang of remorse as she realises it's just the kind of thing Aunty Fiona might say.

'Yes, I did,' Paula says. 'My attention was riveted on it all the time I was giving him instructions about what to do with the minutes of the committee meeting. I do think —'

William suddenly appears between Paula and Alison with glasses of cider in each hand. Both of them blush with embarrassment at their gossip, accepting the drinks with a smile.

'Of course,' June says, 'the Committee seems to be going very well. Miss B is as pleased as punch about it. I heard her merry laugh ringing out behind me on the stairs this morning. Have you ever tried climbing a flight of stairs first thing in the morning carrying two shopping bags, with a merry laugh ringing out behind you?'

'Not that I can recall,' Paula says.

'Well, I don't recommend it. It was a devastating experience.'

'Oh look, there's Mike,' Alison says.

'Really,' June says, 'and who the hell's Mike?'

'Dana's ex.'

They all stare curiously at Mike, who is standing a few feet away, his profile clearly emphasised by the black wall, against which he is leaning. Paula observes the belligerent features and the slow smile playing around his mouth. As if conscious he is being watched, he turns round, a look of irritation flickering over his face as he recognises Alison. It only lasts for a moment, however, for immediately afterwards he grins amiably and saunters over to their corner.

'Hi,' he says, raising his beer mug. 'Skol. You're looking well.'

'Thanks,' Alison replies coldly. She doesn't say anything further, but Mike continues to stare at her in amusement.

'There's no need to glare at me like that,' he says. 'We're reconciled, you know. The little love-nest is once more chirping away.'

'What?' Alison reacts in surprise. 'Are you actually living together again? I mean, I thought Dana was staying with Margot.'

'She was until yesterday. And then we met in the high street and... well, we've reconciled again, as I say... What are you staring at? I thought all your chums would be delighted that we've made it up.'

Alison fingers her glass nervously. 'But, for Christ's sake. Mike, I thought you were through. Dana said the situation was impossible.'

Mike smiles and yawns, looking round to see if his friends are still there. On perceiving that they have moved towards the door, he glances at his watch and begins to shift, as if about to go.

'No, don't evade the issue,' Alison says. 'I thought you and Dana weren't speaking. I thought—'

'God only knows what Dana's up to,' Mike sighs. 'As far as I was concerned, we were through, but she started making melodramatic scenes. To tell you the truth, I think she was becoming suicidal without me.'

'Don't kid yourself. Not Dana. She can manage perfectly all right on her own.'

For a moment the complacent veil on Mike's face dissolves.

'You don't know her as well as I do. In some ways she's very dependent on me. I wanted the whole thing to end, but then she came round to see me the other day and told me she'd just had a bust up with some Polish guy and needed my support, so now we're living together again – until we break up again, that is,' he adds with a wry smile.

Alison stamps her foot, and deposits her cider heavily on the bar counter. 'You make me sick! Don't you realise that it'll be twice as bad for Dana if you separate for the second time? How can you treat her like that? It's so callous!'

Mike looks at the door again and at his watch and making an enormous effort to be polite, smiles and says, 'Look, it's all bloody complicated and bloody sad – and the saddest, most complicated person, as you well know, is Dana. *You* go and argue with her. I can't do a thing with her. She's just attached herself to me again and I'm bloody well involved, whether I like it or not.'

For a moment, Alison's face softens, and the moment Mike perceives this, he smiles cheerily and waving goodbye to them, leaves the pub.

'The bastard,' Alison mutters to Paula.

'Poor Dana. Think what it'll do to her for a second time. If only she could extricate herself from him.'

'The trouble with the liberated woman's wish for self-sufficiency,' William says, 'is that it is contrary to her biological makeup and her essential social, psychological, emotional and environmental inheritance and disposition.'

As it is William's birthday, Alison lets him get away with this twaddle. She purses her lips, picks up her half pint of cider from the counter and swallows it in several angry gulps.

43

Green Stars

'THESE posters are really getting me fixated,' William says. 'I've got to the point where I think of green stars whenever I meet someone from Hull.'

The posters – advertising a forthcoming debate between representatives from the Bridchester Local History Society and history students from Hull University – are dotted with green stars.

Paula, having spent the last half hour worrying about Roger, laughs a little too loudly. 'Yes, I met a woman student from Hull yesterday and I immediately envisaged her as green stars.'

Realising she had repeated his lame joke more or less word for word. she sighs and places two boxes of catalogue cards beneath her left arm and hurries up the stairs to Miss Bushnell's office. As she enters, Margaret appears to be in the middle of a heated discussion with Bert, the caretaker, though as Paula listens it becomes clear to her that neither party is paying any attention to what the other is saying.

'So that's why, in my opinion and after a good deal of thought, I have come to the conclusion that it would be unwise to extend the opening hours to Tuesday. You see...'

As soon as Miss Bushnell pauses for breath, Bert jumps right in.

'I don't mind staying the extra couple of hours – could do with the extra pay in fact. The wife's been very poorly these past few weeks…'

'And why they arrange all this without informing us first, I really can't imagine,' the Head Archivist charges straight on like a genteel runaway train. 'There seems to be no proper channelling of information through the right quarters…'

'Well, it's all right by me. As I say, I'm only too 'appy to 'elp out on these occasions.'

Bert's broad Yorkshire accent contrasts with Miss Bushnell's clipped southern tones and Paula feels as though she's stumbled into a Pinter or Beckett play where neither actor apparently seems aware of the other's existence.

Margaret adjusts her spectacles higher up on the bridge of her nose. 'That's why I get so cross when they do these things without telling me first. You'd think they'd have the courtesy…'

'Delighted I was when they told me about the change. I never mind a change myself. Adds a bit o' fun…'

Miss Bushnell looks up in exasperation to see Paula standing in embarrassment by the door.

'Er, did you want me, Paula?'

'I just came to give you these – I've amended them.' She places the two boxes on the corner of her boss's desk, which, despite her reputation for efficiency, is crammed with letters, books and forms in an untidy heap.

'Oh good. Now that should be a great help.' She repositions the boxes so that they are now perched on top of a precarious tower of books.

The caretaker nods goodbye and slips out behind Paula. Miss Bushnell tut tuts as soon as the door is shut. Despite her outspokenness, the demands of decorum are crucial to her sense of normality and propriety.

'Really, Mr Goodrich is the end. Do you know, he insists on—'

The phone rings and she picks it up wearily. 'Hello, I'll be along after lunch. Goodbye.' She turns back to Paula. 'By the way, did your move go all right?'

'Not too badly. In the end I decided to give up the idea of a flat. It was just impossible to find the right one, so I'm living temporarily in a bedsitter down near the canal. You know, by the sweet factory. It's not too bad actually.'

Margaret's face registers alarm. 'It can be awfully lonely for young people living in bedsitters. You know, you really ought to consider the idea of buying a house or a flat. I mean, your salary is very generous and I'm quite sure you'll feel the benefits of it in a few years. By the time a woman gets to her mid-twenties... well, I suppose I'm old-fashioned but I feel that someone in your position ought to have a proper place of their own. Of course, for all I know, you may be contemplating marriage in the near future...'

Paula stiffens. 'No, I'm not actually,' she replies sharply.

'No, I thought you weren't. The young man I saw you with at that concert, is he—'

'No. That was just an acquaintance.'

'Well, there's plenty of time for marriage. You're still young. Of course, I'm very out of touch with things these days and I don't know what sort of financial arrangements young people make, but if I were in your position I'd seriously consider the idea of buying a small flat. Property prices are quite reasonable here. Now if you were living in London, it would be quite another matter and you know, prices are rocketing all the time. The sooner you put your money into something, the better. I think you'll realise the value of what I've said in later years. How did you—'

The phone rings again. 'Oh dear.' she sighs and picks it up with mock irritation, gesticulating to Paula to leave.

Paula smiles and withdraws quietly from the room. As she is halfway down the stairs she pauses, propping herself up on the blue banister. She has to acknowledge the wisdom of being financially independent as a young woman, which is behind what Miss Bushnell has just said.

For some reason, perhaps because of her aloofness, she has had fewer attachments than most women of her age and she has never deliberately sought the ones she has had. She feels instinctively that she is unlikely to get married in the future, even if she were to meet someone else and she does not relish the thought of a new attachment. She is not in any normal sense involved at the moment. There is only one way out of her dilemma, and that is to break with both Roger and Douglas, so she can be truly independent for the first time for a long time.

The break with Douglas, though painless, will almost certainly involve the greater mental and physical effort, for although she now feels little or nothing for him, she knows how persistent he can be and on his return to Bridchester, he will be appalled to find her feelings towards him so apparently altered.

To end her affair with Roger will involve the greater emotional wrench as neither of them will be able to accept the necessity of breaking up, and yet it is inevitable.

She clutches the thin banister with her right hand and tells herself that by the time she releases it she will have made the decision and will not go back on it. Her hand remains clenched for half a minute and then she lets go.

Heaving a sigh of relief, she sees the two white bars across her palm where the corners of the banister have pressed into her flesh. She runs the thumb of her left hand along the indentations and knows that she will never change her mind.

44

Good Deed

WILLIAM looks hastily around the room of the writers' circle. Much to his irritation, Anna is talking eagerly to Jan in corner.

'I'm afraid your little friend seems to be preoccupied with our Polish creative genius,' Dana says as William sits down next to her, looking disgruntled.

He flushes in anger. He has always disliked Dana: her assertiveness and arrogance annoy him, even though he knows he shares those qualities with her. 'Well, we're all in the same boat.'

'What do you mean by that?'

'Losing our loved ones and all that crap.'

'I've hardly lost mine. I didn't like Jan at all. He just attached himself to me like a leach. He was so bloody persistent I couldn't shake him off.'

'I don't mean Jan – I mean Mike.'

Dana smiles smugly. 'Well, if you must know, we're together again now.' She sits back and yawns peacefully.

'I know.'

'So I've hardly lost my loved ones, as you so delightfully put it.'

'Being together doesn't mean much nowadays.'

Dana stares at him in alarm. 'What do you mean? Have you heard some rumour or something? I mean, he's not seeing another woman, is he?'

'Not as far as I know.'

'So what are you actually saying?'

'Nothing really,' William says offhandedly, at the same time trying to sound as though he's being tactful, which only makes it worse. 'I shouldn't have said anything really.'

'Look, William, for God's sake, stop beating about the bush. Get it out. What are you trying to say? You obviously know something. What is it?'

William sighs and with a mixture of malice and pity says, 'He didn't really want to be reconciled with you. He just felt... well, apparently he felt that you might be suicidal without him and —'

'Who told you that?'

'Alison. He told her in the pub the other day.'

'The bastard.' Dana tries to keep her voice down to a whisper and her throat is almost hoarse in the attempt. 'The lousy bastard. His selfishness is bad enough, but his pity is completely loathsome. How could he?' Her voice shakes as she looks William straight in the eyes.

'I know you weren't trying to be nice when you told me this, because frankly, William, I don't think you're a very nice guy. You were trying to stir things as usual, probably because of your own inadequacies. But as a matter of fact, you've done me a big favour. I felt somehow... I think I knew that he was acting nice, trying to be kind, and I could see through it, but I never acknowledged it to myself.'

She continues to stare at William, who averts her gaze in embarrassment.

'For once in your life, you've done a good deed.'

William tries to laugh, but feels uncomfortable.

'I've got to free myself from him,' she adds, more to herself. 'I've got to get away from his fucking bullshit... he's like some kind of horrible spider, a vicious tarantula, trying to draw me into his poisonous tentacles.'

He chuckles uneasily. 'No need to be quite so melodramatic.'

She laughs. 'I know I can get pretty histrionic when I'm in the mood. If only... if only I could get out of this rut and do something positive. I just feel I'm going to drift and drift, on and on, for years and year, and never get anywhere.'

She looks down at the notebook in her hand and flicks over a few pages. 'I'm not even creative... This poetry – it's not poetry, it's just a few lousy verses. Everyone's churning out this sort of thing. It's not original. I can't go on leading this self-centred, stupid way of life. I've got to *do* something...'

45

Dogs Can't Spell

'MUMMY. Typhoon wants to go out for a W-A-L-K!' Hilary shouts from the garden.

'Don't spell it out – he understands it!' Margot shouts back at her.

Dana settles back in her bath, every muscle of her body relaxing and expanding beneath the soapy water.

'He doesn't! Dogs can't spell!' Hilary persists.

'Ssshhh, don't keep shouting like that, Hilary. It's not very pleasant – and Dana's trying to relax. Now listen. Typhoon can't spell most words, that's true, but he can spell that one.'

'But I didn't spell it. I just said W-A-L-K,' Hilary protests.

At this moment, loud barks from the garden eloquently confirm that Typhoon can indeed spell.

'Now look what you've done,' Margot says, her voice scarcely audible beneath the frenzied barking. 'Now we'll never get any peace this evening unless he goes out... *Tony!*'

Dana hears Margot's heavy footsteps as she goes into the study, which is directly below the bathroom. It is odd how heavily Margot walks. She is not particularly plump, apart from the obvious weight of her pregnancy, and yet she has always had a lumbering gait.

She visualises Margot's large flat feet in thronged sandals moving one in front of the other into Tony's study. This ability of Dana's to visualise clearly the objects within her mind is something she has always enjoyed, and moreover, has always managed to control. It has never intruded upon her external life, but when she is in a certain mood, she can evoke it by an effort of will.

She curls up her feet into two balls and stares at them beneath the grey, soapy water. The slits between the toes appear as cracks, fissures in otherwise perfectly shaped objects. Feet have always intrigued her. She stares solemnly at her toenails as she hears the phone ring.

'Hello?' she hears Margot say. 'She's staying with me. That's right. They've parted for good. No, it's not just a temporary quarrel, I can assure you. Yes, I'll tell her to give you a ring later. She's in the bath at the moment.'

Then she hears Margot laughing loudly. 'Really? I was reading a review of it in the *Gazette*. It sounds horrifying…'

Dana has automatically stops listening as soon as she detects that the conversation has digressed from herself and she acknowledges this fact to herself. She accepts that she is self-centred, but does not feel she is unduly selfish. She can give generously to other people, so long as their views are in accord with her principles. Sometimes this personal morality seems so demanding that she grows weary of it and wonders why she doesn't try to live according to a set code of rules or abandon the attempt altogether.

The process is exhausting and unrewarded. Dana is sensitive to the fact that she provokes a lot of criticism from some people, and sometimes the complexity of her outlook causes her to doubt the validity of her own behaviour in any given situation. At other times she feels assured that this individual effort is not only worthwhile, but also the only possible mode of existence. On such occasions, even when according to external circumstances she has failed, as in her relationship with Mike, she still retains confidence in her own integrity.

Dana can forgive Mike for his boredom with her, his indifference, even his hostility. What she cannot tolerate has been his lack of honesty in his approach to her. She has realised after her conversation with William that Mike is capable of manipulating relationships. Despite her dislike for William, she senses that he is truthful. She is outraged not only that Mike could have imagined her to be totally dependent on him, but also that he should have discussed their problems with Alison. It is not her pride that has been injured so much as the fact that her sense of decency has been affronted.

She surveys her long limbs with satisfaction. She has never had any difficulty in attracting men, but she feels her own sense of inferiority. For some reason Mike despises her, yet he often used to praise her for the depth of her intelligence and sense of judgement. Perhaps the weakness lies in the fact that although she is trying hard to live by her own principles, she is so emotionally dependent on other people. It is this discrepancy that makes her appear so ludicrous to herself, and no doubt to Mike as well.

She ponders on this in turns with a mixture of sadness, anger and finally a kind of wistful self-acceptance. She scrapes at her knee trying illogically to erase a small, grey scar she acquired after a fall playing hockey at the age of fourteen. Remembering, she desists and sighs. Mike has wounded her and nothing can be done about it except to live with it and allow time to heal the scar, although it will always be there.

She switches her hearing back on again to Margot, who is talking to Hilary downstairs.

'So I can make a gingerbread man and give half to Sally for tea tomorrow... Hee hee, that will be fun... Typhoon, come here, you mustn't get in Mummy's way. We're doing some baking.'

Typhoon meanwhile continues to bark.

'I really think I'll have to take him for a W-A-L-K,' Margot laughs.

'You *said* it, Mummy! You said it! You told me not to!' Hilary shouts in great agitation.

Dana smiles. Poor Margot's attempts to talk to Hilary with adult rationality sometimes cause major complications.

46

Strap-Hanging

ANA moves to the right of the bus, feeling highly irritated. She finds it unpleasant enough having to strap-hang in the rush hour without being pressed on all sides by alien bodies. She is acutely conscious of physical contact, which is almost always intolerable to her in these circumstances, more particularly first thing in the morning.

She deftly swivels round her left hand to glance at the time, but find that the face of her watch still hangs downwards, whichever way she flicks her arm. She realises that the strap is slightly too large for her wrist and wonders wryly how many pounds she has lost over the past few weeks as a result of her tortuous conversations with Mike.

She feels an elbow sticking into her back and flinches. The elbow persists; she wriggles angrily back and turns round, a stony glare prepared on her face for the offending intruder, and finds herself face to face with Alison, who laughs heartily at Dana's ferocious grimace.

'My God, you do pull some revolting faces first thing in the morning. If you glare like that at people you *do* know, I'd hate to be someone you didn't know!'

'I guess I'm just a hostile person,' Dana laughs and Alison joins in.

'That reminds me – I wanted to have a chat with you.'

Dana groans. 'Please don't, Alison. I can tell by your voice it's going to be a lecture and I just can't face another one.'

'You sound lousy today.'

Dana grins. 'Gee, thanks. It's nice to know I both look and sound hideous.'

A man standing to her right immediately looks round, as if curious to see someone so singularly dreadful, and after scrutinising Dana for a moment, he turns away again.

'Very demoralising,' Dana whispers. 'Now do give me a lecture, Alison dear. I know what's coming. Everybody has a role to play in society—'

'God, you sound just like William.'

'And I'm neither housewife nor mother nor industrial unit nor creative artist. I'm just a parasite, a nobody.' She sighs.

'Oh do shut up, Dana. You really don't help your situation by castigating yourself.'

'But Alison, what the hell am I going to do? I can't just stay with Margot ad infinitum. I feel I'm sponging off her – I mean, she says she likes having me here—'

'Well, there you are.'

'But I don't know whether she means it. Maybe she's just being polite. Though of course I do babysit quite a lot for her. God, the number of plays I've read over the past few weeks. Do you know, I've really grown to like Shaw. It's odd, because we have nothing in common—'

'Dana, please don't evade the issue. The problem isn't whether you have anything in common with Shaw, it's whether you have anything in common with Mike.'

'Well, the answer to that is definitely no. Gee, I'm crazy. I don't know, I just don't know.'

'The trouble with you, Dana, is you keep criticising yourself the whole time. Don't feel so guilty about everything.'

'But Alison, wouldn't you if you were in my shoes? I just feel like a complete social parasite. I know a lot of people are, but personally I don't enjoy it at all. I mean, hell, what's the point of being a parasite if you don't bloody well enjoy it?'

Alison giggles and as they both start laughing, Dana accidentally kicks the woman in front of her, who moves away indignantly. They look at each other and burst into hysterics.

'Bridchester in the rush hour,' Alison says. 'I hope you'll treasure the memory all your life. One day, when you're a little old granny in some backwoods cottage in Ontario—'

'If only I could go back. If only I could.'

'Well, what's stopping you?'

'The money. And I'm bloody well not going to write home to my mother for the fare back. She's got a lousy enough opinion of me as it is, without my demeaning myself any further.'

'You could always ask your—'

'No, I couldn't. I mean, he'd give it to me, but I've been so bloody unfilial to him. I just couldn't do it – I couldn't stoop that low.'

'Perhaps you could sell him your forthcoming biography of the Duke of Bridchester for the fare home.'

Dana laughs. 'Gee, that's just great. Mind you, there's no need to be so condescending about our great work. It may be unfinished, it may be inaccurate in places, it may be—'

'How much have you written?'

'Not too much of the final draft. We've accumulated a lot of research material and I suppose if someone could be bothered to put it all together, it might even turn out to be an im-

portant original biography of a very interesting historical figure for all sorts of reasons. The trouble is, we all got bogged
down with the source material, all those archives in the records office about rents and tithes, and all the financial minu-
tiae about his philanthropy.

'But that was only half the problem. We needed someone
to manage the project and guide us all, as we couldn't see the
wood for the trees, but since Margot's got pregnant she's
more or less bowed out, and as for William, he proved completely useless – he's more interested in lecturing us all on
what he considers the social evils of the period. And I'm
afraid with everything that's been going on with Mike, I just
haven't had the energy or discipline—'

'What about Anna?'

'Anna? Haven't you heard?'

'No... what?'

'Poor Anna... That Polish jerk Jan gave her the runaround
and then, I'm sorry to say, ditched her and as she was virtually trying to manage the project on her own in the end, the
pressure and stress of it all became too much for her. So...
well, I'm afraid she's had a relapse and has had to leave the
hostel she was staying in... She's back in the Infirmary – she
was admitted yesterday. She rang to tell me and Margot as
she felt bad about letting us down on the project, but she's
got enough to contend with as it is—'

'Good God, I'm so sorry. I know Margot's become very
fond of Anna too.'

'And so was William in his way,' Dana says dryly, her
cynicism mixed with a touch of guilt.

Having made it plain to Jan at Paula's party that she
wasn't interested in him, Dana is well aware that Jan reacted

by turning his attentions on Anna, and it has occurred to her more than once that maybe he was on the rebound when he took up with Anna, which can sometimes be a disastrous way to embark on a relationship.

Moreover, William's feelings for Anna, though clearly unreciprocated, seem to have been genuine and it was presumably because he had been hurt by her rejection that he withdrew his role as Anna's friend and protector at a time when it could well have made a difference.

Alison seems to read her thoughts. 'Yes, poor old William. I know I shouldn't feel sorry for him, but he was obviously quite keen on her before Jan turned up.'

Dana nods in agreement and then shakes her head at the sadness of it all. 'So the bottom line,' she says, 'is that we've all been too caught up in our own affairs to do any more work on the Duke.'

'What you've produced so far – including all the research notes and the primary sources and so on – may not be worth anything scholastically. But I'm sure your father would be interested to see it. I mean, it would show him that you'd done something since you've been here. Seriously, Dana, why don't you show it to him?'

'Just to win his good opinion and cadge the fare home?'

'No,' Alison says, her voice growing taut with frustration. 'You always misconstrue everything I say. You never really listen to people, Dana. That's your trouble.'

'I'm sorry.'

'Look, just show him it. He'll be interested. He might even be able to use it for something. Anyway, the material will be better off in his hands than rotting away in your respective cellars or attics.'

'I haven't got a cellar. Nor an attic. And neither has Margot. I have no idea about William – he probably *lives* in a cellar for all I know. And as for poor Anna—'

'Well, in the murky depths of your mind then.'

'OK, OK, you're right, you've won your case, Alison. I'll admit there's a lot of sense in what you say. I'll tie up all the papers relating to the project in a big bundle—'

'With paper flowers on top.'

Dana chuckles. 'Can you imagine, if I walked into one of his seminars bearing two big carrier bags stacked with all our notes and adorned with flowers. I guess chrysanthemums would be the most appropriate.'

'Why chrysanthemums?'

'They remind me of Bridchester.'

'In what sense?' Alison persists.

'Provincial, gaudy, irrepressibly alive, growing and expanding like the offshoots of a bush.'

The man who had previously turned round to discover whether Dana was beautiful or hideous turns round again and gives her a stare of amazement.

'It's no good, Dana. You'll have to go home soon. This place is obviously getting you down.'

'It's not this place. To be fair, Bridchester is a very decent town. It's just that... I think I need to go back home, Alison. It's the only thing I can do. I've stalled and I need something to get me started again. I'll get the fare from Dad. And I may as well show him all the research project material at the same time. Otherwise it will end up in the garbage bin, like I would.'

Epilogue

THE GREEN and blue chips of stone lie in a scattered heap on the table in front of Anna Crawley as she swivels the urn around between her hands. She has already covered the lower portion with the chips and the top part looks strangely naked without the uneven bulk of the chips. She dips a long green slither into the glue and sticks it onto the top area of the vase with gentle care. It stands out incongruously among the large expanse of brown china.

Anna gazes at it and wonders what adjectives could best describe it. She considers the words 'solitary', 'aloof' and 'absurd'. Then it occurs to her as always that all three adjectives could equally apply to herself in her present predicament.

Today is one of her better days and in the calm silence of the morning, she feel better able to organise her thoughts than usual. And the tranquillisers she has been given at breakfast have chased away the whispering voices that often disturb her thoughts and make it difficult for her to form logical sequences of reasoning.

Dr Gordon has taken early retirement but his replacement, Dr Edwards, has made it clear to her that he would be interested to hear her views on what might be troubling her and causing her to hear voices, but at the same time he does strongly advise her to take her medication regularly.

When her voices come, they seem to bring with them the reward of an extra amount of sympathy and affection, for when she describes in detail her mental and emotional experiences to the doctors and nurses, and after listening patiently for half an hour, nodding their heads in understanding, they show their empathy at the conclusion of the weekly meetings by stepping up her medication doses accordingly, a decision with which Dr Edward is in full agreement.

Her occasional sallies into the outside world are becoming less and less frequent and more and more difficult. No-one except herself understands the fear and the difficulty and for this reason, as well as many others, Anna no longer wishes to be allowed permission out for the occasional lecture or visit to church. Nor does she wish to reassure herself that she can still master her will-power, for she has become weakened by what she terms to herself the pampering of the hospital, and what everybody else terms the necessary treatment.

There is no longer any conflict within Anna between wanting to remain protected yet forcing herself to be independent. Until today Anna has felt as isolated as it is possible to feel; she has felt alone and aloof from the rest of the world and has accepted the fact of her inability to communicate these thoughts to anyone.

She now has a room to herself, instead of being in the open ward she was in during her previous stay. It has a small single bed and a pine wardrobe and a desk at which she can sit and write her poems and through the window that looks out over the grounds she can watch the trees shedding their leaves in the late autumn winds.

In this room earlier today she had some visitors, all of them people she remembered as if from another lifetime. There was a woman in a maternity smock in an advance stage of pregnancy, who looked with kindness and eager curiosity at her through her gold-rimmed spectacles. Anna knew that she knew her and even felt drawn to her, but was unable to reply to any of her well-meaning questions; there was a diminutive woman with a pale face and curly hair, whom she also knew, and whose anxiety and warmth she could sense in spite of her cool, imperturbable façade; there was another taller woman in a yellow miniskirt, who looked like an overgrown buttercup, but who was friendly and chatty and sympathetic; and there was a thin man with a small pale face and long, straggly, biscuit-coloured hair, who talked rather too much, and a lot of what he said was nonsense, but for whom she felt an unaccountable fondness all the same.

She knew that she knew them all and she would have likes to respond to them, but she couldn't, and she sensed their sadness, pity, and embarrassment as if she were watching characters in a television play. And when they left it was as if someone had switched off the television and left her to sit alone in silence. She doesn't mind the silence usually, but today she is not feeling quite as aloof and alone as she had been before the visitors arrived.

She looks again at the single piece of green stone. Maybe she isn't as isolated as she had thought she was, but she is still quite absurd. She does not know why, but she is. There is no denying it, and she doesn't mind that she is, because she senses that everyone is absurd; and as this thought strikes her, she laughs very loudly, so that everyone else in the occupational therapy hut ceases their work and looks up in surprise.

A nurse walks over to her. 'Are you all right, Anna? Are you feeling all right in yourself today?'

Anna continues to laugh, trying to modify the noise but

unable to, so that it doubles in volume.

'Yes,' she says, 'it's just so funny.'

The small, pale face of the young man with the long, straggly, biscuit-coloured hair comes into her mind's eye, and her imagination, always too vivid, is able to transport him onto a horse and make him ride directly over the grass in front of her, gallop-gallop-galloping towards her along the green-green-green grass on his fatal ride, and now she is Grace, and she remembers all his absurd words, dancing like dust and shimmering in the sunlight, and the words dissolve and disappear, but the heart remains, and she feels happy.

The nurse smiles. 'I'm glad you're feeling happy today, dear. What a pretty urn. And what lovely colours. Did you do it all by yourself?'

'Yes,' Anna gasps, wiping a tear out of her eyes that has welled up as usual during one of her laughing fits.

'Well, that's very pretty. We'll have to put it in our display next month, won't we?'